ALL THE PRETTY GIRLS

Cover painting by Bonnie Marin
Edited by Andy Brown
Copyedited by Maya Merrick

Library and Archives Canada Cataloguing in Publication

Mayor, Chandra, 1973-   All the pretty girls / Chandra Mayor.

Short stories. ISBN 978-1-894994-32-3

     I. Title.
PS8576.A958A65 2008   C813'.6   C2008-900808-1

Dépot Légal, Bibliothèque nationale du Québec

Printed and bound in Canada
Distributed by Litdistco: 1-800-591-6250
First Edition

This is a work of fiction. Any resemblance between the characters
depicted here and real people is strictly coincidental.

CONUNDRUM PRESS
PO Box 55003, CSP Fairmount
Montreal, Quebec, H2T 3E2, Canada
conpress@ican.net
www.conundrumpress.com

conundrum press acknowledges the financial assistance of the Canada
Council for the Arts toward our publishing program. The author wishes to
acknowledge the generous support of the Manitoba Arts Council.

ALL THE PRETTY GIRLS

Stories by Chandra Mayor

conundrum press / Montreal

This book is for all the pretty girls I've ever known and loved and hated and cried with and loved some more, but mostly for Karen, the sharpest, most generous, and most beautiful woman I've ever met, the keeper of all my stories.

It is so hot that the features are melting off my face. I am standing at the open kitchen window but there is no breeze, only the complicated sound of Jova's dad picking some blue-grass song on his guitar as he sits on a lawnchair on the hard dirt of the yard. Jova is sleeping and the kids, my daughter Roxie and Jova's daughter Livvy, are chasing squirrels at the side of the house. There is no one else around for miles. Livvy is eight months older than Roxie, they both dance and shriek on either side of their second birthdays, and if they want to chase small animals in and around the rusted out trucks and sedans, the old delivery truck and the hatchback nestled into the skinny trees, that's fine. I'm hot and exhausted and I wipe each plate meticulously, waiting for Jova to wake up.

This precarious house in the middle of the bush is not where I'd imagined being this summer. We're somewhere out-side of Surrey, I'm not sure where. Yesterday Jova's dad, Clive, drove me and the kids around and around in an old pickup, looking at mountains, but I'm still not sure where we are. Somewhere in the middle of bushy nothing, government park land, the back of back. We are guests in Clive's house and he's making an effort, and I appreciate that. He told Jova that I'm a real lady. Jova rolled her eyes and stomped into the bathroom to draw black eyeliner circles around her brown eyes before she went to work. All she does is work and sleep. I've hardly seen her since I've been here, and she's the reason

I came in the first place.

The plan was to fly across the prairies with Roxie curled on my lap, colouring and sleeping. Jova was supposed to pick us up at the airport; she and I had each broken up with our asshole boyfriends, and Roxie and I were going to stay with her and Livvy for two weeks in Vancouver. We were going to buy fruit and coffee on Commercial Drive, walk the kids in their strollers up and down Davie Street, wander around Stanley Park. Stay up all night talking. Find each other's warmth in the darkness and whisper *I'm sorry, I'm sorry* and forgive each other with our lips. I told no one that I'd tucked extra cash, bills rolled tight, into the inside back pocket of my suitcase. I might want to change our return flight. Maybe. Just in case.

But when we landed in Vancouver Mika was waiting for us in the airport, and Jova was nowhere to be seen. Mika helped us find our luggage and told us that Jova had been evicted four days ago and was staying with her dad out in the bush. We stayed with Mika for a couple of days in her tiny apartment, Roxie watching Disney movies in the living room while Mika and I talked in the kitchen. Clive came to pick us up with Livvy on the fourth day and I wondered where Jova was. *Sleeping*, said Clive.

I put the last plate in the green dish rack, drain the sink and wipe off the counters. I pick two kiwis out of the jumble of fruit and joints in the wooden bowl on the kitchen table, find a knife, and peel off their furry brown skin, slice them into soft green cubes and put them on the deck for the girls. I pour stale coffee into a blue speckled bowl for myself, call out the window to see if Clive wants any. He doesn't. I slip an Edith Piaf tape into the open mouth of the boom box on the table, press play, and close my eyes.

Jova wakes up around five, just in time for the pasta salad I've made for dinner. It's still too hot for real food. Clive downs his third can of beer in the last hour, and the girls throw bits of fusilli at each other. After dinner one of Clive's buddies drives up in a rusted red truck; they pop open more beer and start playing duets on their guitars while the kids dance. Jova and I sit on the deck at the front of the house, our legs swinging. She has to go to work in a couple of hours; even though she doesn't have a license, she'll drive into Surrey and take some complicated combination of Skytrain and buses to get to the huge warehouse-type building where she works with forty other women, sitting in a little cubicle with a headset on like the Time Life operator. She's not selling *Dean Martin's Lifetime Collection* or *Ancient Mysteries of the Bible*. She works the 1-900 lines, moaning and hyperventilating into the mouthpiece for four dollars a minute. Of course, she gets paid considerably less than four dollars a minute, but it's a job. The warehouse is not air-conditioned, the cubicles are paper thin and all the girls can hear each other. They finish a call and laugh with each other about the weird stuff the guys wanted them to say. *Give it to Mommy. Oh, your piddle is too big for me.* Jova makes it all sound funny, she talks and talks without stopping, telling me all about the other women, complaining about the heat, assuring me it's the easiest money she's ever made. I know she hates it. Although maybe she doesn't, maybe only I would hate it but she really doesn't mind. I don't know any more. I shift a little so our legs are touching and she jumps up to grab a joint, part of her pre-work ritual. I watch a mouse run along the edge of the house, slip into a crevice. Jova and I get high together, only our fingers touching. I say, *You know that Dan used to hit me.* It's not a question. Jova doesn't say anything at all, only looks up at the still-blue sky, and I don't know what to say next. Jova's hair is bluer than the sky at noon, electric, muppet-coloured, freshly dyed, and I want to touch it. *Nice hair,* I say. *Blue's your colour.* She smiles and grabs one of my long yellow braids hanging out of the red bandana I've tied around my head. *Nice pigtails,* she says, and smiles wide enough so I can see that tooth at the very back that she chipped in the pit at a show two years, an eternity, ago. *I gotta get ready.* The screen door slams behind her and I put my hands against my sweaty face, my cloudy head.

I'm the babysitter here. Also the maid, the cook, the dutiful wife. I'm not sure where Clive gets his money from, some combination of the vehicles and parts out front and the marijuana field in the back. I try to keep the kids out of his hair during the day, even though he seems to spend a considerable amount of time every day playing his guitar and drinking with any one of the men constantly stopping by. At least he notices. *Thanks, doll,* he'll say whenever I make food or sweep the kids around to the front of the house. I don't know who watches Livvy when I'm not here, who'll watch her, feed her, play with her when I go home. Livvy and Roxie spend their time drawing in the dirt with sticks, following bugs, scraping dirt into plastic pails, and falling off the rusty swing set in the front. I feel like I'm trapped in some hillbilly movie. There's a woodstove in the living room. None of the furniture has legs. The kids are grimy all the time. No matter how often I make them take a bath together, their tans and the dirt have turned both of them as brown as nuts. I chase after them outside, jam hats on their heads to protect them from the sun, feed them raisins and fruit and Cheerios. I read them stories at bedtime and they fall asleep all tangled together; I stay up late every night reading but I'm always asleep before Jova gets home and falls into her own bed two rooms away from me. She works all night, sleeps all day, and I'm so lonely. I can feel resentfulness creeping into my voice, my fingers, all the secret, hopeful corners in me.

It's evening again, days later, I'm not sure how many. Clive's out somewhere. He rattled off in the brown Honda and I'm not sure when he'll be back. The girls are digging for beetles in the wood pile outside, and Jova and I are in the kitchen. She carefully stubs out a joint in the ashtray, puts the roach away in a little tin box. We're always stoned, a long smooth glide, my words thick and slow. *How's Winnipeg?* she says. Lonely, I want to say. Scary. *It's okay,* I say. *Different. Everything's different now. Dan keeps calling. But I've got a court order. I don't know. Where's Jake?* She lights a cigarette, talks out of the side of her mouth, rolls an orange lighter between her fingers. *Who cares*, she says. *He's living with some chick on the Island. She's a controlling bitch and she's got a kid of her own so he never sees Livvy. Whatever.* Heartbreak hangs in the air, unspoken. And fear. And relief. *Remember that party?* she asks. I know which one she means, at the big house off Sargent. It got totally out of hand in about an hour. She used a bat to run off a bunch of guys dealing bad PCP because her roommates were too scared to do anything about it. Jake left for more beer and never came back and I held her on her little bed upstairs while she cried. We drank vodka and locked her door and kissed, and the music thumped and the floor trembled. It was our first time and someone rattled the door but we didn't get out of bed until we woke up, limb to limb and bathed in sunlight, hours later. *Sure, I remember,* I say, my chest tight. *Those stupid fuckers*, she says, laughing. *Remember? I ran those stupid fuckers off with a bat.* Sure, I think. You sure did. I turn my head away, hating the dope in my brain and the scratching in my eyes. *Jova*, I say, staring out the window above the sink, the greenness of the tree leaves hurting my eyes. *Jova, did anyone tell you? I mean. I came out. After Dan left, I like, came out.* My hands are curled into fists on my lap, and I can't look at her. I can hardly breathe. She takes a long drag on her cigarette and starts digging through her purse for something. *Hey, that's cool,* she says. *Meghan sits beside me at work. She's a dyke. Lots of the women at work are dykes. What do you think the kids are up to?* She gets up and walks to the bathroom, lipstick in hand. *Can you check on the kids?* she asks over her shoulder. *Make sure they're still alive out there.* The door closes behind her. I keep staring out the window, motionless. The blue sky taunts me. It stays light so long in July and I wait and ache and wait for the darkness. I get up to check on the kids, start getting them ready for bed, and half an hour later Jova drives away, beeping the horn as she turns left at the mouth of the driveway, lost in the trees.

On my last day, Clive slips me forty dollars as I'm packing my old black suitcase. *No,* I say. *Thank you, but that's totally unnecessary.* He makes me take it anyway. *Just in case,* he says. *In case the little one needs something. Jova!* he hollers. *Jova, get your fucking ass out of bed and say goodbye!* A few minutes later Jova stumbles into the living room, bleary, makeup smudged around her eyes. I'm trying to explain to the girls what's happening. *Bye-bye,* I make them wave. Bye-bye. *Hey,* Jova says, sits down on the ratty couch and pulls Livvy onto her lap. Livvy squirms away and runs back to Roxie, puts her arms around her and the two of them stand in the middle of the room, hugging. Roxie pats Livvy's long black hair, breaks out of the hug, looks around the room and comes running back with a pink hat, puts it backwards on Livvy's head. I light a cigarette. *Hey,* says Jova. *Come on outside for a minute.* We walk out onto the deck, and she uses my cigarette to light one of her own. *I can't believe you're leaving already,* she says, staring at the trees. I watch her profile as she blows smoke up into the air. *I'm just so fucking tired all the time. I hardly saw you.* I think about the words I'm going to say. *It isn't what I thought.* She looks at me, then looks away again. *Me neither,* she says. I wait for her to say something else, but she doesn't. Behind me I hear the kids start to yell and screech; they're fighting over a toy, a doll that belongs to Livvy that Roxie's trying to stuff into the suitcase. I go inside and give the doll back to Livvy and promise Roxie one of her own when we get back home if she'll just cool it and give me a break. I'm tired. My empty stomach clenches and I'm tired deep inside all my bones. Clive said he'd give us a ride to the airport in Vancouver; he says he doesn't mind the long drive there and back again. We throw the suitcase into the back of the truck and I pile Roxie in, lean in to do up her seatbelt while Livvy stands beside the truck and cries. Jova's still standing on the deck. Livvy runs up to her and wraps her arms around Jova's legs as we pull out of the driveway. The blue sky drifts around the house and the tops of the trees like a postcard, snapped fast in my mind.

Kate needs a nanny for Charlotte, who is three years old and sunny and wild. I need a job and I need to get out of my apartment, away from my boyfriend. I need women in my life and Kate is six years older than me, a lifetime. I sit at her kitchen table, the wood gleaming in the morning sun, drinking coffee. I smoke cigarettes and stir spoonfuls of dark brown sugar into my pink mug because Kate says that's how she made it at the expensive coffee place where she used to work and it seems a luxurious secret, like knowing what to serve with couscous. There is so much that I need to learn. Charlotte plays under the kitchen table while Kate and I talk. Kate tells me all about her recently imploded marriage to Nathan. I know Nathan; he and my boyfriend Chris play video games together and I have been to the house he rents on Ruby Street, a shabby blue place with a Wiccan ring made of white stones on the tiny front lawn. Kate made it and Nathan left it there. I'm not sure what it means but I'm too embarrassed to ask. Kate tells me about their Taoist wedding ceremony, about how she was late and Charlotte threw a tantrum. Nathan isn't Charlotte's real father and he never officially adopted her because Kate's still hoping to get child support from Charlotte's dad even though the courts can't find him. Kate and Nathan share Charlotte at the moment and I know Nathan loves her because I've seen her over at his place and he holds her and reads to her and never seems to get impatient. But Kate tells me that he undermines her, that he says bad things about her to Charlotte, that she can't trust him. I sip my coffee and think about how everything is so much more complicated than it seems. I worry about Charlotte under the table, listening to everything we say, but Kate doesn't seem concerned. Maybe Charlotte doesn't understand what we're talking about anyway.

The phone rings and Kate jumps up to answer it. It's Aaron, the guy she's sort of seeing. He lives in Kenora and he's a Marxist and he writes poetry. She met him at a party. I ask Charlotte if she wants to watch Mr. Dressup. She smiles and nods and her pigtails bounce. I ask her if she likes Casey or Finnegan better and she tilts her head to the side and puts her finger in her mouth. *Who what?* she asks me. *Casey*, I say. *And Finnegan.* She's looking at me like I'm speaking a foreign language and I don't know how else to ask the question or what else to say to her. She watches me with round brown eyes and her little eyebrows raised and I think, I'm going to be terrible at this, and I can feel the tips of my ears flushing pink. Kids are a mysterious species of their own, with their own language and customs and rituals and I don't understand any of it. I turn on the TV and flip through Kate's four channels until I find Care Bears in French. Charlotte curls into a corner of the couch and ignores me totally.

Kate's still on the phone with Aaron and they seem to be arguing about something; I'm trying not to eavesdrop but it's hard not to hear. I decide to do the dishes. I don't know what else to offer to this apartment of tiny pink boots and abandoned butterfly hair clips, gleaming wood and yellow curtains, Mucha prints on the walls and Mexican blankets on the couch. I find the dish soap and the dish rack in the cupboard under the sink. I carefully wipe each cup and bowl, the inside and the outside. I'm much more thorough than I am at home. At home I'm careless and rushed and I just want to get it done and over with and Chris is always freaking out about lipstick smudges on the glasses and bits of food stuck to the pots. Chris is always freaking out about something and at home I live in a constant state of apathy and anxiety. Resignation and panic. But I want to do a good job for Kate, I want her to smile and say, hey, thanks, and I want to come here every day, starting Monday morning.

I lean around the corner to check on Charlotte but she's utterly absorbed in the pink and yellow bears and doesn't notice me. I bring her a little plastic glass of apple juice but she just waves her hand without looking at me so I put it on the coffee table. Behind me I hear the phone slam down; Kate picks it up and slams it down twice more and disappears into the kitchen. I stand frozen beside the coffee table and then I hear her crying. A friend would go to her; that's what women do for each other. I hold my breath and walk to the kitchen doorway, lean against the solid wood frame. Kate's head is on the table, nestled in her arms. Her shoulders lift up and down in time with the small muffled sobs. *Kate?* I say, feeling large and clumsy. I walk over to her and put my hand on her shoulder. I want to put my arms around her and say all the right things, but I'm not sure what those things are. Instead, I rub a small circle on her left shoulder. *That stupid fucking asshole,* she says, lifting her head. Her eyes are red and her cheeks mottled. *Stupid,* she says. *Fucking. Asshole.* I fill a glass of water for her from the kitchen sink, put it on the table beside her arm. She drinks from it and wipes her face with her sleeve. I'm not sure if I should touch her again, if that helps her at all, if that's okay or not. I don't know what she needs from me. I sit on a chair and pick at my sleeve. *What happened?* I ask. *He's not coming,* she says. *He was supposed to come this weekend and we were going to go to the Windsor to see this band, and now he says he has to work and can't come to Winnipeg.*

The Windsor is a blues bar. When I lived downtown I used to go there in the afternoons to drink cheap draft, but I've never been there at night. Chris only wants to go to the Albert to see hardcore bands play and I always go along with him. *That sucks,* I say. *But if he has to work, it's not like he has a choice, right?* Kate looks at me like I'm an idiot. *He doesn't really have to work,* she says. *It's that slut Emily. His ex. He's going to spend the weekend with her, I know it.* She looks out the kitchen window onto the alley. *Did he say that?* I ask. She scrapes her hair back from her face and starts pulling it into a braid. *Didn't have to,* she says. *I just know it. Sometimes you just know. Why do I always get involved with assholes?* She reaches into the pocket of her jeans, pulls out an elastic, wraps it around the end of the braid. *Asshole,* says a small voice from the doorway. I look and see Charlotte standing there, watching us and picking at her nose. *Asshole,* she says again. *Slut.* Kate puts her head back down into her arms. *Oh my god,* she says. *I can not handle this right now. I can not deal with any of this.* I look at Charlotte who's now hopping up and down on one foot. I can see her mouth moving. Slut slut slut, she mouths. Kate's shoulders are starting to heave again. *Do you want me to, like, take her to the park or something?* I ask. *Oh my god*, says Kate, lifting her head so I can see the tears on her cheeks again. *Please. Get her out of here. Take her to the fucking park.* Charlotte jumps and starts spinning. *Fucking park, fucking park*, she yells. I get Charlotte's pink jacket from the peg by the door and hold it out for her to stick her arms into. She stops jumping and holds her arms straight out from her body. She looks at me and whispers, *fucking park*. I fit the sleeves over her arms and whisper, *No, Charlotte. Don't say that. Say, happy park. Happy park.* She looks at me and tilts her head to the side. *Happy fucking park*, she whispers.

As I'm fitting yellow rubber boots onto Charlotte's feet, Kate comes and stands in the doorway. *Thanks*, she says. *Really. And I guess you're hired.* Pride and relief swell through my stomach and I can feel a stupid grin spreading across my face. I bite my cheeks to hide it because I don't want to smile when Kate's so upset. *Listen*, she says. *Fuck that stupid asshole. Do you want to come to the Windsor with me on Saturday? It'll be cool.* I think about Chris; this Saturday he wants to go see some friends of his play their first show. It'll be awful but he'll freak out if I don't go. I decide I don't care. He'll be mad but I can handle it. *Yeah*, I say. *Sure. Sounds like fun.* Charlotte is pulling at my hand, reaching for the doorknob.

Did you hear that? I ask Charlotte as we walk down the hallway of the apartment building and start down the stairs. *We're going to play together every day. We can go to the park every day*

if you want. And we can watch Mr. Dressup, and Casey and Finnegan.
Charlotte is pulling at the front door. I turn the lock above her
head and open it. *Okay,* she says. *Casey who?* I grab her hand
as we step outside. The park waits for us across the street,
muddy, with patches of dirty snow huddled around the poles
of the swing set. *Casey,* I say as we cross the street. *And
Finnegan. My favourites.* Charlotte runs to the swings. *Mr. Slut!*
she yells. I look up at Kate's bedroom window behind us, but
she has the curtains pulled shut and I can't see anything.

Saturday night I meet Kate at the bus stop on Portage. I'm
wearing a short black skirt and fishnets and red heels. Kate
shows up in jeans and a flowing white shirt with blue embroi-
dery across the front and I feel stupidly overdressed. *No,* she
says. *You look hot.* On the bus she tells me about the book she's
reading, Julian Barnes, *The History of the World in 10½ Chapters.*
She says it blows her mind. I wish I had a piece of paper so I
could write it down before I forget. When I go to the library I
just stand there looking at all the shelves of books and feel totally overwhelmed. All Chris reads are books with warriors and
wizards, stupid things that make my eyes ache and glaze over
just thinking about. I want to know what Kate knows. Kate
says that everything is fine now with Aaron; she called him at
work and he answered so he wasn't with Emily after all.
Unless, I think, Emily was at work with him. But I don't want
to ruin this night so I don't say anything.

The Windsor is crowded with people and hazy with
smoke, and Kate finds a table full of people she knows.

They're all a little bit older than me and they all look totally at home here. The band is already playing so she yells in my ear that she'll introduce me during a break. We dump our jackets on chairs and pull our purses crossways over our shoulders and Kate grabs my hand and pulls me to the floor in front of the stage to dance. I've never danced to this kind of music before; I know how to hold my own in a pit but I'm not sure what to do with my arms and legs here. Kate is swaying her hips and dancing and the bass player looks down at her and winks. I try to copy what she's doing and pretty soon I think I've got the hang of it. Some guy starts dancing with us and at first Kate smiles at him, but when he starts getting too close and aggressive and I start feeling uncomfortable, Kate grabs my hand and turns me around so that my back is facing him. She gives him the finger and then laughs and focuses all her attention on me, and it's like the people dancing all around us are invisible. I can feel the music all the way inside me now and we dance through four songs, and then the band stops playing and the set is over. We go back to our table, and Kate introduces me to everyone sitting there. She doesn't call me the babysitter; she introduces me as her friend Molly and everyone nods and smiles at me. I don't remember any of their names but it doesn't really matter; even without the music it's still too loud to really have a conversation. The waitress comes by and we order beer, in bottles, not draft. I'm glad to be here, with Kate and her friends. I'm glad not to be at the Albert with Chris, even though I'm sure he's going to be mad for at least a week that I didn't go with him. But it doesn't matter that much because I'll be at Kate's during the day anyway, hanging out with Charlotte. And maybe sometimes when Kate gets home she'll invite me to stay for supper and I'll eat vegetarian stir-frys and organic salads and pumpernickel bread instead of Kraft Dinner and Zoodles. And she'll tell me about books and Marxism. Maybe I'll tell her about Chris, about the stuff that happens at home, and maybe she'll have some advice for me.

The waitress brings us our beer and I sip mine slowly. I'm thirsty from dancing but I only have money for two beers so I want to make it last. Kate and her friends are talking around me and I tip the bottle to my lips, let the cold liquid flow slowly down my dry throat. When the band starts playing again Kate jumps up to dance and I go with her. It's two in the morning before I get home; Kate paid for a cab and said, *See you Monday morning, sugar* and I still don't feel like sleeping. Chris isn't home yet. He'll probably go to a party after the bar closes and won't come home until morning. I can't wait for Monday. I lie in bed staring out my window, until the tops of the trees begin to glow softly in the dawn light, and eventually I fall asleep.

When I get to Kate's apartment on Monday morning I can hear Charlotte's crying all the way down the hallway, and I can hear Kate yelling. No one answers my knock, but the door is open so I go in. *Charlotte!* Kate is yelling. *Charlotte, you're a bad girl! You're a bad lying girl!* Charlotte and Kate are in the bathroom, and Kate is holding a bar of soap. *What's going on?* I ask. Kate turns around. *I've fucking had it,* she says. *Nathan called this morning, and Charlotte answered the phone. He asked her what she did on the weekend. What did you tell him, Charlotte? Hey? What did you say to Daddy?* Charlotte is crying and she looks up at me with big watery eyes. She says something really quiet. *What?* says Kate. *Say it, Charlotte. You didn't have a problem saying it ten minutes ago. Tell her.* Charlotte cries and looks up at me and she is like a bird I saw once with a broken wing, hopping around and dragging the wing. *Said,* Charlotte sobs. *Said Mommy fucks Aaron.* Kate grabs Charlotte's arm and forces the bar of soap into her mouth. *Dirty, bad, lying girl!* Kate yells. *Why would you say that to Daddy?* I'm confused and scared. Kate looks at Charlotte, sitting on the toilet with the bar of soap jammed in her mouth and says, *Now I'm going to be late for work. And Daddy's never going to talk to you again.* She slams out of the bathroom and I can hear her in her bedroom, stomping around and banging her closet door. I take the soap out of Charlotte's mouth and she just looks at me, tears spilling out of her eyes. I pick up her Bugs Bunny toothbrush and squirt green toothpaste on it, help her brush her teeth to get the soap taste out of her mouth. She spits out the foam and I put more toothpaste on the brush, tell her to brush again like a big girl. I hug her and she nods. I tell her I'll be right back and walk out of the bathroom, closing the door behind me. I'm trembling and my stomach is clenched. I go to Kate's bedroom, watch her zipping up her skirt. *Why are you so mad?* I ask her. *You are sleeping with Aaron, aren't you? Why are you so mad at Charlotte? She's really scared.* Kate sits down at her vanity and starts jamming the little brush in and out of the mascara tube. *You don't fucking understand, Molly*, she says to me. *Nathan and I are supposed to be working on our marriage.* I put my hands in my pockets to hide the shaking. *But you said your marriage was over. I don't understand.* She doesn't even turn to look at me. *It is over,* she says. *But Nathan doesn't know that. He thinks we're working on it. And if he knows I'm with someone else, which thanks to Charlotte he now does, he won't do this with me anymore. How do you think I afford everything?* she asks me. *I can't fucking afford this apartment and Charlotte and you and food and everything on my own. Nathan gives me money. And now he won't. Unless I can convince him that Charlotte is lying. She might have wrecked everything.* I want this not to be happening. I don't want to think about Charlotte in the bathroom, brushing her teeth, and the bar of soap with little tooth marks in it sitting on the edge of the tub. *But that's not fair,* I say. *Charlotte didn't do anything wrong. That's your secret, not hers.* Kate stares at me. *Fuck fair,* she says. *What's fair? Is it fair that I'm stuck in this stupid city with a kid and a failed marriage without a cent to my name? Is it fair that I gave up everything for my stupid kid and my stupid ex and now I have nothing of my own except my clothes and some furniture I got at the Sally Ann? And what about your welfare ass? Is it fair that you sit around all day and do nothing and my taxes pay for that and then I have to pay you again so you can spend the day watching TV and fucking around in the park with Charlotte?* I can feel my eyes burning, I can feel my cheeks turning pink but I can't say anything. *Whatever,* says Kate. I shrink against the door frame as she walks past me. *Whatever,* she says. *Stay today. I don't care.*

But you're fucking fired. Don't come back tomorrow. I'll find someone else to sit here with Charlotte. She grabs her coat and slams the apartment door behind her, and she's gone. I push my hands into my eyes to try to stop the tears.

Charlotte is still in the bathroom. She's still sitting on the toilet holding the toothbrush. She looks up at me and says, *Mommy's mad.* My hands are still shaking. *Yeah,* I say. *It's okay, Charlotte. Do you want some apple juice? Do you want to go to the park?* She nods her head. *Happy park?* she asks. *Uh huh,* I say. *That's right. Happy park.* I get her jacket and her boots on, grab my own jacket, and we walk down the stairs and across the street to the park. At first she just sits in the swing and dangles her legs, but after I push her a few times she gets into it. *Higher!* she shrieks, and I push her as high as I can. Some other kids show up and she spends an hour running around on the play structure with them, laughing. She falls down a couple of times but she doesn't seem to care. The other kids leave with their moms and Charlotte wanders back to where I'm sitting on the red wooden bench. *Apple juice?* she asks. I say, *Sure, kiddo, let's go home.* I scoop her up under my arm and she giggles. I don't know what's in her head; I don't know if she's forgotten what happened this morning or if she doesn't care. Maybe she's used to it. Maybe she's just taken it and put it somewhere else in her head where she doesn't have to look at it. I do that. I don't know if kids can.

Back inside the apartment I settle Charlotte on the couch with some apple juice in a Sesame Street glass and a plate of crackers with Cheez Whiz on them. I found the little jar of

Cheez Whiz in the very back of the fridge, behind the goat cheese and the rice milk and the grapes, and I thought that today is a Cheez Whiz day. I turn on the TV and find some kids' program I've never seen before. *Look, Charlotte*, I say. *Look at the dog. Isn't he cute?* Her eyes are glued to the screen. *Blue*, she says, her mouth full of cracker crumbs. I don't know what she means but I let it go. I've just settled into the couch with my legs folded up when the phone rings. *Hello?* I answer. It's Kate. *Hey*, she says, and her voice is bright and sunny and light. *Hey*, she says again. *So, like, I totally overreacted this morning.* She laughs. *I'm a mess without coffee. I'm a regular Medusa.* She laughs again. I don't say anything. *I didn't mean anything I said. You're not fired. You're a total sweetheart. Forgive? Friends?* I don't know what to say, but my hands are shaking again. She's waiting for me to say something. *Yeah*, I finally mumble. *Yeah, I guess. Sure.* Charlotte is watching me. *Let me talk to Charlotte*, she says. I hand the phone to Charlotte and say, *It's Mommy.* She takes the phone and holds it up to her ear. *Mommy?* she says in a little voice. She smiles. *I love you too, Mommy*, she says. There's a pause, and she says, *Happy park. And crackers.* She pauses again and then says, *Okay, bye-bye.* She hands the phone back to me and I put it to my ear and say, *Hello?* but there's no one there. Kate's already hung up.

The dog show is ending, so I pick up the remote and flick through the channels. When I flick back to the dog show channel I hear the theme music for Mr. Dressup and so I stop there. I remember being little and sitting in a square of sun on the floor at my mom's house, drinking apple juice and watching Mr. Dressup. I'm glad it's still on the air. I'm glad it's on right now. *Look, Charlotte,* I say. *Mr. Dressup! Quick, who do you like more: Casey or Finnegan?* Charlotte looks at me and doesn't say anything. She looks back to the TV. *Annie!* she yells. *Granny!* I look, and there are two new puppets dancing around on the screen, a little girl puppet and an old woman puppet with grey hair. I think that they've expanded the puppet community. That's nice, I think. But we watch the whole show and Casey and Finnegan never show up. They've been replaced, I think, and feel the way I would at a funeral or something. Or more like three days after a funeral you never even knew about, when you run into someone and they say, *Yeah, my grandma died. I thought you'd come. She always asked about you. Why weren't you there?* Stupid, I tell myself. I'm in mourning for puppets. And Charlotte's really happy, so what do I care? But I wish we'd never watched the show. I wish I'd never found out that everything is different. I get up and make myself some coffee in the kitchen and I can still hear the show on in the background. I go back to the living room and pick up the brush from the coffee table. Charlotte climbs onto my lap and I brush her hair out, shiny and brown and smooth.

CARLY'S HIPPIE MOFO SHIT: MIXTAPE REVISITED

1. VINCENT (STARRY STARRY NIGHT)

We know, quite clearly, that the world was never meant for ones as beautiful as us. I use Comet on the kitchen counters and Windex on the bathtub because I'm kind of an idiot in the world. When you see what I've done you shake your head in exasperation. I hold myself very still and my breath rakes sharp fingernails of shame inside me. And then you laugh and say, *Oh, who the fuck cares*, and I smile and breathe and all the tiny fingernails are torn away. I hand you little bits of me, pink and shiny, on fingertips and the glowing tips of cigarettes. *Carly*, I say. You turn your face toward me over your shoulder, your small body crouching on the floor, rearranging your albums — alphabetical, chronological. *Yeah?* you ask, a strand of Joey Ramone black hair caught in the corner of your cracked lips, smiling. *I don't know*, I say. You turn back to your albums, the plastic sleeves sticky under your fingers. *Me neither,* you say, laughing. You sit beside me on the couch at night, wrapped in the pink and green quilt my mother made for me. It makes my stomach clench with uncertainty every time I look at it. We stare at the back of the billboard standing sentinel outside our window. We don't know what it promises on its glossy face, anniversary rings or humming furnaces or just women frozen with their lips lit and lifted up in scripted joy. We only see its scarred and latticed secret back, hunched forward into the world, braced, blocking the light. I think I know what's in your own dark pink heart, but I don't, not really. You go home to Windsor over Christmas, and when you come back, you tell me that your friends aren't who you thought they were, that they are lame and stupid. You tell me you've realized that I'm really your friend. *Dumbass*, I think. *Took you long enough.* All your records are pristine, and all mine skip. The black discs, the thin arm moving inexorably into the centre of the red plastic stereo, the only things moving for hours at a time. We open the wooden apartment door with the black grate and let in the things that bruise us, things that laugh and leave slushy bootprints on the floor and pass out in my bed. I watch you across the room, and in the centre of you are very small things that I only have too-big words for. Red cords of hope. Longing. Uncertainty.

The song abruptly starts playing about a quarter of the way in because I never really knew what I was doing with the tangible things of the world — countertops and ashtrays and stereo buttons and faces that stretch into smiles as if there are no pools of danger inside with hungry open throats. I can't remember now exactly how it begins.

2. WALK ON THE WILD SIDE

We shift and shimmer, flickering inside our own variable skins. Even our faces and the contours of the ridges on our fingers seem inconstant, mercurial, ready to slough away and reconstruct themselves as something different, untraceable, unrecognizable, at a moment's notice. One evening we wrap ourselves up in our ratty second-hand coats, the worn fabric and our own bodies too thin for the steely unblinking cold air outside. We slip next door to the Fort Garry Hotel, the limestone glowing in the moonlight like the underbellies of mushrooms and snails, the blank-eyed stone women pressed close to the windows stacked twelve storeys into the air, the green-streaked metal roof disappearing into the sky. The rooms cost a million dollars a night, and the bellboys wear uniforms. This is where the queen sleeps when she drops out of the empire-sky into this tree-pinned prairie city with wide streets built for oxcarts and flat-eyed men asking for change. This hotel is where the ghosts live, everybody knows it, and Carly and I are hungry for ghosts, for life as ephemeral and quicksilver as our own, but also for something that lingers and can't be sent away. We tell the bellboy at the front door an elaborate story about ourselves, a rickety matchstick construction of obvious lies, and we are bold and compelling and brazen. We believe that he believes us when we tell him that we're grad students in parapsychology doing field work at nine on a Tuesday night, and that only he can help us, right now, tonight. We are, after all, very young and very pretty.

There are secret underbellies to this hotel, networks of amiable young men in red jackets who pass us off, one to the next, as they take us through the maze upstairs, the back stairways and service elevators, the dark rooms where ghosts have been spotted over the years. The gilt-edged mirror where the weeping young woman appears to unsuspecting guests, the deep plush of the eighth-floor hallway carpet where disembodied footsteps are heard at night, the seventy-year-old echo of hobnailed boots on wood planks. A bellboy opens one of the forbidden doors to the roof, and Carly and I step out into the gateless night, eyes bright for the flash of white wrapping around a gable, a fleshless hand caressing the ear of a gargoyle.

One boy checks to make sure that no one's watching, and leads us down a back stairwell into the basement, and from there we descend further into three layers of sub-basements, rotting stairs that we're warned about, cobwebby rooms full of cast-off furniture, gloom, and menace. Carly and I are awed, silent, and our new bellboy friend laughs. We are deeper in the earth than we've ever been, waiting for the whole thing to collapse on our heads. We find a cellar with black dampness streaking the walls, visible only by the glare of a bare bulb on a cord. *Someone was tortured here*, we agree solemnly, and scared out of our minds, Carly and I hold hands. *Let's go home*, I whisper in her ear. *I'm so done here*. She nods and we smile at the bellboy and make him take us back upstairs and laugh and laugh and thank him and won't give him our phone number when he asks, not because we don't like him, but just because we don't have a phone.

At home again in our apartment we talk about everything we saw, and every time we tell the stories they are more elaborate, more bewitching, populated with stranger and stranger sounds and premonitions and foreboding feelings and inexplicable things glimpsed out of the corners of our eyes. We believe ourselves absolutely, and it is a great relief: we always knew there was something dark running through our lives, something terrible and compelling, some reason that we pulled away from love in ways we couldn't understand or explain. And if it lives next door, in the unused rooms and secret sub-floors and forbidden roof and dirty cellars, we know where it is and where it calls from, and it can't, it just can't live inside our own unknowable hearts.

3. Moonshadow

Are you going to stay the night is a question I rarely bother asking. Somehow Kevin is abandoned with me in the apartment, his friends and my friends gone off somewhere. Maybe it's a setup. I'm very good at this, I've discovered, and I don't know exactly why, but I'm hungry all the time. *Tell me I'm real*, I say in my head. I move my thigh against his on the couch, pretend not to notice his startled face. I lean forward for a pack of matches and let my shirt slip off my shoulder. This is a scene I can play out in my sleep, and yet my pulse jumps underneath the thin skin at my wrist, because he could always say no. I feel his fingers, soft, uncertain, at my waist. They press awkwardly into the pliable skin, and I am suffused with tenderness for this boy that I am seducing. I let him lead me through this diminutive dance, turning, encouraging, making small practiced noises when he falters, when he's not sure what to do. This is his first time, and this is a small gift I am giving him, gifting him to himself. What I get is that he won't forget. The girl that I am at this moment will live on somewhere other than in my own imperfect memory. And perhaps his memory will hold a lovelier, surer, more beautiful version of me than I can carry myself.

When it's over, and he and I are smoking cigarettes in Carly's bed, I say to him, *So, is it Kevin or Kyle?* I know, of course, that it's Kevin, and I will always remember this moment, his hand playing in my hair, the ashtray resting on my legs. But he doesn't need to know that. And it's important that I let him know where things stand.

4. PEACE OF MIND

Only Canadian kids of a very small and particular generational moment listen to The Grapes of Wrath. Mersy and Colette come over with a bottle of Southern to christen the apartment, and we play a shots game with pornographic playing cards from the early 70s that Carly stole from her dad's basement closet. The bottle is empty in half an hour, and Mersy and I decide that going to the Blue Note is an excellent idea. Of course, once we get there we realize that it's actually a very bad idea. Crossing through the parking lot on the way back to the apartment, I fall on my face over and over again, except it doesn't hurt at all, and Mersy and I think that's so funny that we both fall again, the October pavement cool against our purple cheeks.

Colette and Carly have gone to the Spectrum, half a block away. Too drunk to walk, they sit outside with their backs against the brick, trying to cajole passersby into giving them a ride home. Two guys in pickup trucks offer them a ride in exchange for a blowjob, and suddenly they remember how their legs work. At home, Carly is moaning for Mikey, the Spectrum DJ. Colette leaves to find him, and when she returns, she looks down at herself. *Have I taken any clothes off since I got back?* she asks. We look at her torn white Ramones T-shirt, her laddered black nylons. She has been wandering the world in a T-shirt and pantyhose, and everyone has seen her bunched and flowered white cotton panties shining beneath the sheer black nylon, the thick elastic at her waist. *No*, we say, and her face falls. Which we also find hysterically funny.

Between the four of us, we've seen just about everyone that we know. And the ones that we don't see will hear about it the next day anyway.

At some point a girl that Carly knows, from a band that's just about to hit nationally, shows up at our unlocked apartment to check on us. She throws out a plastic garbage can that one of us has puked in. We've all passed out, so she finds blankets and wraps them around us, leaves a bottle of Tylenol conspicuously on the table beside the pictures of big-haired soft-breasted women.

The world isn't that unkind. It's just us who are unkind to ourselves, over and over again.

5. FEMME FATALE

Nico's husky voice coils through the rooms of the apartment. Carly and I have clear roles in the eyes of our circle. She is frigid. I am the slut. No one seems to have time or words for anything more complicated than that. Carly develops a fixation on Marcus. We call him the Sun King for his long, white-blond hair. She makes a plan, and everyone, everyone except Marcus himself, knows about it. He comes over on a Saturday night, and we all make excuses and leave, reconvene at the Blue Note. Alone with the Sun King in the apartment, Carly has put on mascara, borrowed one of my skirts. These seem to be necessary accessories. They play a couple of records, and he fidgets. She tries to look alluring, and he asks if she's okay. She stubs her smoke out and reaches for him, kisses him hard on the lips. He looks shocked, stands up, reaches for his jacket. *I have to go*, he says. *Wait, don't go*, says Carly. *No, I gotta go*, he says. He is almost at the door. Carly is frantic. *You can't go*, she says. *I told everyone that I was going to sleep with you by Sunday.* And then she can't believe she's said that. No one will believe she said that. He turns around slowly. *What am I?* he asks in indignation. *A piece of meat?* And Carly can't help it, and starts laughing as he slams the door on the way out.

We all pile back into the apartment in a couple of hours, eager to find out what happened. Carly is back in jeans, sitting on the couch, smoking furiously. An argument breaks out: who's the bigger idiot, Marcus or Carly? And then we start talking about something else, and smoke a few bowls, and finally everyone else leaves. Alone in the living room, Carly turns to me, jabbing the air between us with her cigarette. *You have to sleep with him*, she says. What? *I don't want to sleep with Marcus! He's so pale and skinny. He looks like he crawled out from under a rock*, I say. *No*, she says. *You have to. If you can't sleep with him, no one can.* And this is true, at least to us, at least in that moment. *C'mon*, she says sweetly. *I'll give you a bowl of Froot Loops if you do.* And I say I'll think about it. I pretend that the Froot Loops — Carly's most prized food group, the one I've been banned from because she says I eat them too daintily and don't slurp enough — is the motivation. But it's not. It's Carly. We don't know the word solidarity. We do the best we can.

A year later, I'm spending the night at Carly's new place, and Marcus shows up. There's not much going on, and I convince him to linger in the living room with me. It's easy to let him think it's all his idea, and it doesn't take very long. After he dresses and leaves, I wrap a blanket around myself, and bang open the door to Carly's room, where she's sleeping in bed with her new boyfriend. *I believe*, I say dramatically, *that you owe me a bowl of Froot Loops.* It takes Carly a minute to figure out what I'm talking about, and then she turns gleeful. *You didn't!* she says. *Oh, I did*, I say. She jumps out of bed and makes me the biggest bowl of cereal I've ever seen, in an orange mixing bowl. She feels vindicated. She feels proud of me. It's enough.

6. SOMEBODY TO LOVE

Sometimes we laugh at ourselves, listening to music made before we were even born. Music that even our parents never knew. Sometimes we head out to the Spectrum, fling ourselves around to Gorilla Gorilla and Red Fisher. Sometimes we spend an evening on the couch, immobilized by hash, shouting over Suicidal Tendencies. All of this will end soon anyway, except we don't know it at the time. Almost twenty years later I'll sit in my best friend's apartment in another city, find an old cassette tape and a stereo that still actually plays such things. I'll remember choosing each song because it meant something, though I won't always be able to remember what it all meant. I'll misremember things and get it wrong and knowingly make things up out of nothing. In the end it will bear little resemblance to anything that ever actually happened. And it'll all be absolutely true.

7. IF YOU WANT TO SING OUT, SING OUT

Carly lives in the top of a house a block away from me. Her name's not really Carly, but it doesn't really matter what it is. She's back in Winnipeg after fifteen years away, and we can't find anything to say to each other. There are small malnourished ghosts of us at the bus stop up on Portage, singing this song, not caring who hears us. Being free looks different than we thought it would. She gives me a bracelet she bought on eBay, tiny elasticized panels of the Virgin Mary. I bake her a Red Velvet cake for her birthday, and it doesn't turn out at all the way I thought it would. The colour is rich, like bread soaked in blood, but it doesn't have much taste. We take a long time to eat it, and then we watch TV. I think maybe the ghosts are more real than we are, now. I think maybe we just can't even hear each other. I can't figure it out.

8. TEACH YOUR CHILDREN

There's an old acoustic guitar in the corner of the apartment. It's missing a string, but we've learned to play around that. We've decided that there isn't much you can't play with A, E, and D chords. My throat can only find the notes if someone else is singing with me, but Carly's voice is husky and true. James comes over once or twice. He's older than us by twenty or forty years; at this point in time we can't really tell the difference, and we don't care. He's gentle and kind and makes me think of Leonard Cohen. He sings this song with Carly, encourages her to take the harmony. Their voices together make wings in my ribcage, make the edges of this room drop away into nothingness. Make me forget to breathe. Carly's black hair hangs over her face, hiding the yellow bruise on her eye where she talked me into punching her so she'd look tougher. I couldn't bring myself to hit her very hard and I didn't do a good job of it; when I wanted to try again she said it hurt too much and wouldn't let me. James' long fingers tap his knees, and as he sings, we both watch Carly. Sometimes it really is as simple as this. Two voices. A broken guitar. A fragile thread of hope. One slightly shattered girl at the other end of the couch, listening.

9. BOTH SIDES NOW

My suitcase packed in the corner behind me, toothpaste and lip gloss in clear Ziploc bags, I hit play one more time. There's more left on the tape, metres and metres of iridescent black cellophane wound tightly around the tiny wheels in the cassette. The steady thrum of the crackling guitar fills the room, and the little orange cat looks up from her nest on the unmade bed. I sit cross-legged on the scratchy carpet in front of the stereo, lean my head against the LCD screen where tiny green slashes rise and fall with the music. I let the words and the music, familiar as my own heartbeat, nestle inside the black wool of the little jacket on my shoulders, slide along the strands of my hair that I dye brown to cover the occasional streak of silver, all pulled back haphazardly with sharp black pins. Just for a tiny moment, I let myself wait for my sixteenth birthday again, caught up in the youthful fragility that knows that all the words of all the songs are truly about me. The illusions of all the girls that looked like Carly, all the girls that looked like me, all the ones who believed that we'd already seen both sides of everything. There's a woman waiting for me at home, a woman who loves me but finds that after ten years I'm not really what she wants at all. There's a child, a girl with a sketchbook and great pools of light and shadow in her eyes, walking the tightrope through her own teenage years. There's a woman in an upstairs apartment down the street, listening to records late into the night. All those bruised and laughing girls, smoking cigarettes and playing broken guitars in downtown apartments who feel the things that they lose pull at their fingertips, every day. It still hurts and sparks and lingers, in the way that only ghosts can. What I have now is substantial and thrumming with blood, my own self sitting in my familiar body, my heart softer and stronger, less mysterious to me. A ticket in my pocket, a plane to catch. The fragile wisps and steel edges of hope, well-worn and comfortable in my cupped hands.

ZOODLES IN THE AFTERNOON

Zoodles kills babies. Those bright blue cans in my kitchen cupboard, three of them, with pink and yellow animals leering from the labels, represented three dead babies. Probably. I wasn't actually sure of the tin-to-baby ratio, but every time I cranked the can opener along the Zoodles rim, I'd condemned another enormous-eyed, swollen-bellied baby to powdered formula mixed with contaminated water. My grubby little kitchen swelled with the wavering, grief-soaked presence of dark-skinned mothers, weeping for their dying babies, their arms wrapped around themselves, accusation burning into the back of my neck. I sat down on the cracked red vinyl of a kitchen chair, the tin with the can opener still hanging off it on my lap, let my head fall back on my neck until the skin on my throat stretched taut, and felt tears gather in the corners of my eyes. Mucus began to settle in my nose. The cooked Kraft Dinner noodles sat on the stove in the green pot, cooling, clinging to each other in starchy embraces, waiting for the slick red tomato sauce to slip inside all the pale hollow throats.

"Food ready yet?" Devon called from the living room. I didn't answer. Any possibility of my own voice was drowned out by the tiny mewling of the babies, held tight in their mothers' thin arms.

"Food?" Devon asked again, sticking his head around the corner. I put my head down on the table. Tomato sauce from the half-opened can seeped through the metal slit, rubbed against the front of my T-shirt like smears of blood.

"Oh, sweetheart," I heard Devon say. "Is it the babies again?" I felt his arms wrap around me from behind. I nodded, my forehead scraping against the plastic ridges of the tablecloth. The tablecloth was patterned with pink and orange martini glasses with geometric cherries and lemons. It wasn't exactly the right shape and hung over the edge of the table almost to the floor, but it had been $1.99 at Dollarama, and I thought it would be cheerful. Devon hated it. He thought it was froufy. I thought it was worth it just to hear him say froufy. It made me feel like I was Holly Golightly with a ridiculous tiny tiara perched on my head and he was the writer-guy, the one person I could rely on, entirely bewitched and enchanted by even my silliest gestures.

Someone told me that the book was really different from the movie. Darker, sadder. That Holly wasn't actually a Hepburnesque icon of femininity and loveliness, but a very sad, shattered woman. I never want to read that book.

"And the women," I said in a muffled voice. "The mothers are here today too. Oh god, it's awful. It's so awful. I just can't."

He reached under my breasts and took the can. I heard him step toward the counter, heard the grinding of metal on metal as he cranked the opener around the rim. "Mags," he said. "Sweetheart. There are no babies. There are no mothers." A spoon scraped against the ridges of the metal tin, rattling like a train over uneven tracks. I heard the splash of milk, the clank of the spoon against the edges of the pot as he stirred the Zoodles and milk and cheese into the noodles. I felt him put a bowl down in front of my head. It was a little decadent to eat Zoodles and KD together; that was two dinners worth of food. It was a treat. He was trying to give me something silly and sweet and just a little bit special. My throat closed up and I reached out and pushed it away. He sighed.

"Seriously, Maggie. Every time, with the babies."

"And the mothers," I said.

"Fine, and the mothers. It's just Zoodles, for fuck's sake." He didn't sound angry. Exasperated, maybe. We'd been over this lots before. "Mmmm, cheesy tomatoey goodness," he tried. I tried to sniff the snot back up into my nasal passages, an ugly, rattling sound. "Look, babe," he started.

"Don't say *babe*. Don't say *baby*." One part of my head knew that I was being ridiculous. One part of me could see, like I was looking down from the ceiling. Two bowls on the table. Pot in the sink. Devon's shoulders tense in frustration, his eyes soft and blue and turned down at the corners. Trying. Me, head down, hair hanging all over the place, crying over imaginary babies I'd never even seen except on Christian Children's Fund infomercials at four in the morning. *What's wrong with you?* I asked myself. But the grief seeped through my bones like heavy black smoke, pinning my body to the chair, my arms to the table, my head to my arms. The smell of the Zoodles / KD mixture made me feel like vomiting. *One more thing*, I thought. *I can't take one more thing.*

"You know, we didn't buy the Zoodles," Devon said. "They're food bank Zoodles. We didn't, like, participate in the economic whatever." He tries, he really does. He didn't read newspapers, just fantasy novels and music zines. He and his friends hung out at the Albert, the dingy punk bar downtown. Drinking draft all Saturday afternoon, staking out their places before the bar set up a cover charge for the night. I hung out at Mondragon, the vegan anarchist co-op bookstore and restaurant just up the street from there. I mean, I wasn't really part of the crowd. I knew who most of them were; the couriers, the socialists, the writers, the queer activists, the girls with long, long dreads tied up in beads and scarves, flowy beige or mossy green pants made out of hemp or bamboo or something, sweat-shop free sneakers on their delicate feet. They just seemed so focused, so sure, so electric. They were like lean, bright candles. I felt like there was something missing in me, some spark that would let my mouth open in front of them, propel my tongue into asking questions, slow the crazy percussion of my heart long enough to offer an opinion on something. Mostly I just borrowed books from the shelves and flipped through them, reading snippets here and there, making my one fair trade cup last as long as I could. Just trying to figure it out.

"It doesn't matter if we didn't actually buy them ourselves," I said. "We're still participating in the systemic economic and cultural colonization of under-developed nations." I lifted my head to look at Devon. *Please understand*, I thought. *Please stand up and dump out these bowls, please explain to me how to make this work, please help me heal the babies and the silent mothers and my own stupid, stupid heart.* "I just… I can't eat this. I'm sorry," I said, putting my head back down.

"Okay, Mags," Devon said, and I felt his hand reach across the table and settle on my hair, heavy and warm and smelling a little like cigarettes. "I'll just stick it in the fridge in case you change your mind later."

He was so good to me, still. The first time we'd met, I'd been sitting on the cracked wooden steps outside Mondragon, smoking. He was walking by, and stopped to ask if I had an extra cigarette. "Tailor-made," he'd said. "Awesome." Usually I rolled them with a little black machine that went *shh-chuunk* as it pushed back and filled the crinkly paper tube with tobacco, but the day before I'd decided to splurge on a real pack. I'd taken them out of the red cardboard and put them into the plastic square that I kept the rollies in, so no one would notice how decadent I was being. I was surprised that this guy had noticed right away that they were real smokes for a change, and then I tried to explain that I didn't usually buy them. And then I thought I sounded pretentious, so I tried to explain that I wasn't actually trying to hide them. And then I realized that I wasn't really making any sense at all and that this guy really didn't care what the hell kind of cigarettes I bought or didn't buy, and then I felt my face turn what I knew to be a particularly unattractive shade of mottled dark pink, and then I stopped talking in mid-sentence. *Very, very smooth*, I'd told myself. *Really, well done.* But he'd just laughed. "I happen," he'd said, "to have a real eye for quality." And then he'd winked.

It was a stupid line. It was lame and dumb and cheesy. But it kind of got me. In real life, no one's as smooth as they are in the movies. No one gets that many rewrites and retakes in the real world. And I'd appreciated that he'd made the effort to say something nice, to lay something light and kind over the big awkward space I'd made. I'd liked the way he was watching me, not predatory, not contemptuous, just easily waiting for me to say something more. Like he'd had nowhere else to be. I'd felt my cheeks cool down to a normal shade of pink, and I'd laughed, and he'd smiled in response. His eyes were blue and tipped down at the corners, but when he smiled they tipped upwards just a little, and I'd thought, *I did that*, and something delicate and ferocious inside me had flared open a little at the edges, like sand dollars and tiny petals, like a glowing curl of bark in a fire just before a spark leaps out.

"I've been thinking about loons," I'd said.

"Loons?" he'd asked, smiling. "Like, the birds? Or the neighbours?" He gestured with the cigarette I'd given him down to the end of the street, where some guy was yelling and waving his arms at a lamppost. A car drove by on Bannatyne, and a scruffy bike courier I vaguely recognized gave me a weird look as he bumped past me up the steps into the building behind me.

"Forget it, it's dumb. I'm sorry," I'd said. "Look, you probably have to be someplace. I'm sorry."

"No, hey, I like loons," he'd said, sitting down beside me. "Seriously. My brother can do this awesome loon call with just his hands. When we were kids at my uncle's cabin we'd sit out on the dock at night and he'd make this crazy loon sound, and after a couple of times, damned if there wasn't an answer. Like, from some other part of the lake. It was kind of weird. Spooky. What made you think of loons?"

"You sat on the dock? Did you have a motor boat?"

"Nope," he'd said, watching me and smiling. "Just a canoe, loon-girl. I'm pretty good with a canoe. I'm Devon."

"Maggie," I'd said. "I just, I heard this thing. This thing that Margaret Atwood said."

"Who's Margaret Atwood?"

Who was this guy that he didn't know who Margaret Atwood was? But he was still sitting there, still kind of smiling, still doing that tippy thing with his eyes. "She's just this writer. Canadian writer. I was named after her."

"Are you a writer?"

"God, no," I'd said. "Words are —" I'd waved my cigarette around in the air. "Words are complicated. I... I draw things." He'd waited and smoked and watched me. "Sometimes," I'd said slowly, feeling stupid and brave and a little breathless and a lot reckless. "Sometimes I draw boys."

It took him a minute. Less than a minute, thirty seconds maybe. And then his eyebrows popped up into his forehead and a big grin made the tops of his cheeks round and soft and something electric seemed to slip through his lean frame. He'd given me a slow appraising look and I'd felt like a dancer under a spotlight on a stage, just at that moment before the music starts and everyone is holding their breath. He'd flicked the ash off his cigarette, and I'd noticed that he smelled clean and sweet, that his shoelaces were two different colours, that his hands were wide, the nails short and square and scuffed.

"Tell me about the loons," he'd said. "No one's ever told me anything about loons before. Robins, check. Grackles, budgies, chickadees, yup. I'm all ears for this." He'd sat beside me, stretched out his legs in front of him.

"Okay," I'd said. "Okay. It's kind of... well, it's kind of nothing, really, I guess. I was just thinking about this thing I heard. That pretty soon there won't be any loons anymore. Margaret Atwood says that it's the motor boats, on all the lakes. That they fly around the lakes, and they're so noisy, and there's so much, like, wake or whatever behind them. And it all washes onto the shore, in waves, over and over. Like, *whoosh, whoosh, whoosh*." I'd lifted my arm out to the side, drew it over and over again in the air in front of me, like the waves. He'd kept watching my face.

"Yeah, okay, I know what you mean," he'd said.

"But see, that's what the problem is," I'd said. "That's where the loons make their nests. On the shores of the lakes. And then, like, the waves from the boats wash the nests away, with all the eggs inside them. Or, god, baby birds inside them. All those little baby loons, they just drown in the water. They never get to grow up. They just... they just splash around, in the water, and the water's too much for them, the waves are too strong." *Oh god*, I'd thought. *Stop, Maggie. Stop talking. You're wrecking it.* But the words had kept slipping out. In the middle of the afternoon, sitting in the middle of the warped wooden steps, this boy had opened up this little space between us as if he held it cupped in his hands. And I'd liked it a lot, and now I'd started falling into it and I couldn't stop.

"And they fight it, and they really try to swim. But they can't, they're too little. And they just die." I'd known that I was talking too fast, that I wasn't being funny or quirky anymore but kind of unexpectedly crazy instead. I'd felt my cheeks begin their hot pink burn again. Another car drove by, and all I could hear was the engine, louder and louder in my ears, drowning out any other sound on the street. And my ears had filled up with another sound, a wet kind of thunk, the sound of tiny tendons and insubstantial little feathers sodden with dark water, parchment-thin skin like my own eardrums stretched around tiny bones, beating, beating weakly, and then giving up, sinking. And when I'd tried to look out at the street through my own eyes, everything was sheened in water, distorted and shimmering wetly.

"Hey, hey there, big-heart girl," I'd heard the boy beside me say. He'd reached out and started rubbing my upper arm, softly, up and down. Gently, like he'd thought I'd shatter. "Swear to god, I've never been in a motor boat. Bastards, those boat drivers. Pinprick dicks, all of them. That's why they make such a big noise. Nothing in their own engines, if you know what I mean." I'd heard the smile in his voice. *I'm such an idiot*, I'd thought. *What am I doing? I'm sitting on the fucking street crying, for chrissakes.* "Here, have another smoke," he'd said, taking one out of my own pack, lighting it and handing it to me. "Now me, I'm strictly a canoe man. Friend of loons the world over." He'd grinned, and leaned back, and raised one eyebrow in an exaggerated leer. "You should see my J-stroke sometime, sweetheart."

It was so silly, and so sweet. I'd started to laugh, rubbing at the tears in my eyes with the sleeve of my hoodie. The street sounds had started to come back, the normal ones: the guy still at the lamppost up the street, leaning in now and talking low in a cajoling kind of voice; the cars with just a normal engine rumble; some band doing a sound check over in Old Market Square across Bannatyne; the low mutter of conversation drifting over from the patio of The Line-Up across the street. The dying baby birds had just sort of faded away, and I'd felt, with a small sense of wonder, the late afternoon sunshine on my face and hands. The faded blue of his jeans bunching softly around his long legs, still stretched out beside me, had looked achingly soft, like I could plunge my hands deep into the fabric and curl up in it, fall asleep. *He's still here,* I'd thought in amazement. *He's still talking to me.* I'd turned to him and smiled, a small smile, hope lifting the corners of my lips, looking right into his eyes. He'd blinked.

"How about a drink, Maggie?" he'd asked softly. "I happen to know of a very fine establishment right up the street from here. Best draft in the whole city. Cheapest, anyway. And excellent patrons. All canoeists. Maybe a kayaker or two. Not a boat driver among them. Promise."

He'd stood up, and held out his hand. I took his hand, and he'd pulled me up to my feet. The easiest thing in the world.

That was months and months ago. Almost a year. Many, many small lifetimes.

"Maggie!" Devon shouted from down the hallway. "Mags, I have excellent news for you." He reappeared in the kitchen, grabbed a chair, scraped it across the floor until it pushed up against mine. He took my chin in his hand, turned my face toward his. I looked into his shining blue eyes, and the ghosts of the women behind me turned toward him too. "Sweetheart. I looked it up on that Wikipedia thing. It's fine! Honest. It's Nestle who makes the baby formula in Africa or whatever. You know, the chocolate people. Heinz makes Zoodles. No one's boycotting Heinz. They're like the ketchup kings. Zoodles don't kill babies. Kit Kat kills babies. I hate Kit Kat. You hate Kit Kat. We'll never eat Kit Kats again. Zoodles, Zoodles we can eat until we explode!"

The women behind me flickered a little. They turned to each other and muttered. "Wikipeda is crap," I said uncertainly. "They don't fact-check. Anyone can write a Wikipedia entry. I could write a Wikipedia article about, like, the cancerous properties of dandelions or something. And everyone would just believe it because it's on the Internet."

"Okay, but I went to the Heinz site too. I even looked at the corporate governance part. There's nothing about Nestle anywhere. Honest. See, baby, it's fine. We can just, you know, have lunch together. C'mon. C'mon, sweetheart." He cupped his hand around my cheek. *He tries so hard*, I thought. *He really means it.* His hand was warm against my face. The tips of his fingers were callused, and scratchy against my skin. I flashed to a quick snapshot in my mind from last night. Devon sitting on the yellow plaid couch, smiling at me, playing the guitar, the metal strings caught between the wooden neck and the pads of his fingers, his other hand stroking the taut strings floating over the open hole in the body. He was warm and solid and leaning towards me like there was nothing else in the world.

"Corporate structure is super-complicated," I said. His eyes drooped a little, and he took his hand from my face, leaned back in the chair. He turned away from me and looked out the window. I began to talk faster. "All these companies, they're basically owned by like seven people in the whole world," I said. "It's totally incestuous. And they don't put any real information on the Internet, because then people would know. They deliberately hide how they're all in each other's pockets, how they're all basically the same thing. I'm sure there's a link. I read it somewhere, for sure. I just...."

My voice trailed off. He wasn't looking at me. *Oh god*, I thought. "Devon, please," I said. "Please. I'm sorry. Thank you for looking it up. Really. It's just, you know. The babies. I can hear them. I know that's dumb, I know it's stupid. But I can't help it." I reached out my hand toward him, but I couldn't make myself actually touch him, the soft blond hair on his arms, his bony shoulder under the orange T-shirt.

"The babies, Maggie. I know. The fucking babies." I felt my eyes begin to itch and burn. "It's just, it's always the babies. Or whatever. The polar bears. The... the sea kelp. The kids in Cambodia. The fucking dolphins." He lifted his hand, shoved it through his hair. The tiny cowlick at his hairline flattened under his palm, and sprung up again. He turned to look at me. "I love your heart, Maggie," he said evenly. "I really do. I love your big, soft, bleeding heart. I love that you love so much. I just.... Fuck it. I just need some too. I need some room for me in your heart. There are no babies in this room. There's just me and you. Me," he said, his eyes glassed with moisture. "Remember me?"

I looked at him, sitting just a few inches away from me. I wanted to get up and throw myself into his arms, curl up in his lap, pull his scrawny arms around me, close my eyes and breathe that combination of sweat and soap and cigarettes and slightly stale laundry that was just him, the smell that I curled into every night in bed. But I just couldn't. I felt the ghosts behind me shimmer and start to fade away, like after you blow out a candle and the thin line of grey smoke burns your nose for a minute, and then is just gone like it never happened. I was alone again in the kitchen, alone with Devon. My fingertips twitched, wanting to reach for him, but he may as well have been on the moon. My pulse thudded in the back of my head like angry waves slapping the shore, and I couldn't move.

"When was the last time you drew something, Mags?" he asked. I opened my mouth to answer, and then just closed it again. I wasn't sure. In the beginning, I used to draw all the time. That first day, when we'd met each other in the street, we'd gone to the Albert and hung out with his friends and laughed and played pool and everything was bright and sunny, even inside the gloomy falling-down bar. And then we'd slipped up the street to Subway for something to eat, and it hadn't even bothered me that the chickens were all factory-farmed and the lettuce was covered in pesticide. We'd decided to try subs with every possible free option on them and could barely fit them into our mouths. I'd drawn a loon for him on a paper napkin and he'd laughed and folded it up and stuck it in his wallet.

It was still in his wallet. I saw it last week when I went looking for change to have enough for the hundred mile bread at the bakery. This raggedy bit of cheap paper napkin, carefully folded into a corner. I'd unfolded it and saw that he'd written my name on the back, and the date of that summer day in his careful clumsy printing, five hundred lifetimes ago. And I'd cried.

I hadn't even opened my sketchbooks in ages. I used to draw things all the time, leave them around as surprises for him. Tiny sketches of birds with candles, trees blossoming with stick insects, scrawny boys with snowflakes caught in their disheveled hair. And I used to draw things for myself, too. Whenever it got too much, whenever anything hurt or just felt too damn much, I drew something, and the sweep of the pencil across the thick paper pulled something out of me, caught it and tightened it and transformed it into something else. And then I could close the book and put it away.

But there are some things that you can't draw away. Or at least, I couldn't. There are some things that are just gone before your pencil even knows what they look like. The things I was drawing got sadder and darker. Big trees with thick knots that looked like butterflies with their wings half-pulled away. Bits of shells, and bits of things that used to live in the shells. And things that looked like babies. Things that whispered in your blood all the time, unexpected things that might have tipped down eyes. Things you never knew and couldn't find a shape for. Things that made you really see the world in all its devastation and horror. How all those starving polar bears, skinny and wretched on melting ice floes, all those little insects and birds slipping away forever in faraway jungles, all those flesh and blood people stepping on leftover bits of metal and rage forgotten in the ground and feeling half of themselves torn away in one tiny second of inattention, how all of it, all of it, killed you before you even began. How it's just no world for babies, even the ones we don't poison on purpose.

Back in September, after it happened, we'd replaced the mattress, bought new sheets, new blankets, new all of it. And I'd bought the stupid tablecloth, and a long long necklace of fake green plastic pearls, and a sweet black dress in a very small size that I never expected to fit into so soon. And a big pack of coloured pencils. But now I still can't sleep and I can't eat and I can't stand the feel of the dress against my skin. And the ghosts in the kitchen are way more real than me.

"I gotta go," Devon said, pushing his chair back. "No," he said, looking at my face, skin pale, my mouth open like a fish. "No, I don't mean it like that. I'll be back, Mags. I keep coming back to you, crazy girl." He smiled, but it didn't look very convincing. "I've just gotta go for a walk or something. You know, out in the real world. I've just gotta.... Oh hell," he said, and ran his hand through his hair. "The thing is, Maggie." He looked at me, steady and still. "The thing is, you can't protect every damn thing. You just can't."

I didn't say anything, and my hand moved, almost on its own, almost without me even noticing, to sit lightly on my belly, right over the tomato smear, the smear like blood.

"I'll be home later," he said. I heard him walk down the hall, grab his jacket off the peg behind the door. The door opened and closed, and the lock clicked as he turned his key from the outside. The old floorboards of the building creaked under his footsteps in the hallway. I heard the muffled thud of the fire door, and then nothing.

I sat at the kitchen table, filled my ears with the silence around me. I got up, ran some water into the pot in the sink. *Stupid, stupid idiot*, I thought. *I should make a card or something*, I thought. *I should make a card and put it on his pillow. I should...* and I sat down again at the table.

"How do you get up every day?" he'd asked me once, when we were lying in bed in the morning sun, and I was explaining to him about clothes made in sweatshops, about young girls with long nimble fingers, about accidents and blood and over-seers like something out of Dickens and union busting and EPZs and how there was nothing, nothing I owned that I could possibly put on my body without drowning in the blood. "How do you get up and walk through the world every day, Mags?" he'd asked, trailing a finger up and down my bare arm. "Something's gotta give, sweetheart," he'd said, grabbing me and rolling me close to him. "Open up, marshmallow.

Open up and let something go, just for today. Open up and let me in." He'd teased the edges of my lips with his tongue, and I had, I'd opened my mouth to him and I'd opened my whole self to him, the puddles of blood around the piles of T-shirts and jeans in the corner fading away into nothingness.

I put my head down on the tablecloth with the stupid fruit stamped on it and cried as the room smudged into violet-edged twilight around me. *Idiot*, I thought. *Moron. Stupid, stupid girl.* I can't protect every damn thing. I know that. I can't even protect one damn thing. One small, precious, drowning damn thing. The tap dripped, and the jagged voice of a crow cut through the sky outside the window. I got up to get some toilet paper from the bathroom to blow my nose. I listened for the door. I felt a shimmer and shift in the air behind me, and I didn't turn around. I waited for Devon. I just waited.

FUCKING ON WRECK BEACH

"I heard about this place on Ruby."

"Yeah?" says Em, flicking the filter of her cigarette with her thumb. I watch the ash fly past the plastic blue bench we're sitting on, past the brown plastic garbage bin on her right, into the thinning bushes. It sits like an offering on a flat green leaf that's browning at the edges. I take a moment to track my kid, pink pants, green shirt, jumping on the rattling suspension bridge on the play structure. Em's kid is watching her from one of the square wooden levels beside the bridge. She's just sitting there, swinging her legs. She's too far away to hear us. There are about eleven kids at the playground today. Twelve, if you count Jayden, standing as usual on the edge of everything, not moving, watching the rest of the kids with blue shuttered eyes. He's like the children of the corn. He gives me the creeps. Em and I are the only moms around.

"I saw an ad on the pole by Cousin's. It's a sublet. $475 a month. I can swing that if I quit smoking," I say, digging in my purse for the piece of paper with the phone number on it.

"You're not going to quit smoking."

"Whatever. I could. You're such a bitch. Anyway, I could probably do it anyway."

"How many bedrooms?"

"Just one. But I could sleep on the couch, right? I mean, whatever. I've slept on worse."

Em laughs. "Steve and I slept on Wreck Beach for a whole

summer. Sand is fucking hard."

"So a couch is no big deal."

"Your couch smells like cat piss."

"Ha ha. Hilarious. You've slept on my couch."

"It'll be the end of your sex life," Em says, drawing on her smoke again.

"Melanie and I broke up, remember? I have no sex life. Anyway, you've fucked on couches. I've fucked on couches. You, apparently, fucked on Wreck Beach."

"Everyone fucks on Wreck Beach. Everyone should fuck on Wreck Beach at least once in their lifetime. But only once. Fucking sand, man." She's laughing again.

"I did it on a beach once. Victoria Beach. And I did it with that guy, Mark, remember him? We did it on the riverbank. I don't actually remember much."

"I remember Mark. I was at that party, dumbass. It wasn't Mark. Mark had the skinny legs. You went off with Jesse. He was the one with the blue hawk."

"Shut up! I did not sleep with Jesse. I would totally have remembered sleeping with Jesse. I would have remembered the revulsion. I would still be able to taste the revulsion. I would still be showering today, for fuck's sake. Jesse. Dirty. Never."

This is how all my conversations with Em go. We start off talking about one thing and end up talking about something completely different. We usually start off talking about how to get out of this hellhole. Everyone who lives here talks about how to get out. It's our favourite topic of conversation.

Subsidized housing. We all wanted in. Now we can't wait to get out.

And we usually end up talking about the old days. Not that they're so old. But after you have a kid, it feels like several lifetimes ago. And I also feel like that girl I used to be is sitting on the other side of me, listening in, waiting for a chance to jump in, acid in hand. And I can see the ghost of Em sitting on the other side of her, waiting to chase the acid with Johnny Walker. No one knows who I am anymore except maybe Em. She's sitting here with me, anyway, in this shitty playground outside our shitty Furby apartments, me upstairs, her down. Watching our kids. Smoking cigarettes. Talking shit. The usual.

"It doesn't matter," Em says. "You were only gone for about ten minutes. Nothing much could have happened. He was probably too drunk to fuck."

"Gross. Maybe. I just remember the tree limbs. Lifting out of the ground." I smooth down the front of my skirt. I've started wearing 70s bridesmaid dresses. If I have to shop at the Sally Ann I'd rather not look hideous in high-waisted khaki shorts and worn-out old Disney T-shirts. All the other moms think I'm a freak. A bra-burning feminist kissing-girls-in-the-elevator dyke freak. It works.

They talk to Em, though. She knows lots of the women in the building. And trust me, it's pretty much all women. The only man around is the caretaker, a cranky old fuck who's supposed to be around all the time, but really only bothers to show up for a few hours every couple of days. He yells at us for leaving butts on the ground by the playground bench. We make a desultory show of picking them up and putting them in a pile on the bench between us, like we're planning to throw them into the garbage bin, then as soon as he's around the corner of the building we knock the pile onto the dirt again. Whatever. It's not much of a rebellion. Actually, it's pretty childish. And I guess one of the kids could eat one, and that would be bad. But most of these kids are pretty clear on what cigarette butts are. And somehow, life gets really small when you live here for a while. Everyone's got more power over your own life than you do — like the welfare workers, prone to dropping by unannounced and banging on your door, even though the rules say that they have to make arrangements in advance of a home visit. But if you try to remind them of that, they just smile and threaten to cut you off. Or, you don't hear from them for months, even when you need something and you're calling every damn day, leaving messages. *Do not leave more than one message*, their answering machines always say. *Calls will be returned as soon as possible. One message is sufficient.* Yeah, right. I have the numbers for a bunch of underfunded, understaffed anti-poverty, welfare advocacy groups in my address book, and every now and then I give them a call, check with them about some of the rules and regulations. Sometimes it helps to know how things are actually supposed to work. But mostly, the workers just do whatever they want. Because they have the power. And we don't. And everyone knows it.

The only other men we see much around here come by on Friday nights. Daddy Weekends. Not all the kids have daddies, and even then, a lot of them don't bother. Still, it breaks up the week. Starting at about six every Friday evening, more cars than normal line up along the street, men sitting in the driver's seats, usually honking. And then the parade of moms and kids, backpacks hanging off their scrawny little backs, trooping down the front sidewalk, looking for the right car. There aren't any dads in the picture for Em and me and our kids, but, at least when the weather's okay, we like to settle ourselves on the bench on Friday evenings anyway. We bring peanut butter sandwiches and travel mugs of coffee and sippy-cups of juice for the kids, sometimes fruit if we have it. Concessions for the UWV Showdown — Unsupervised Weekend Visitation, usually court-ordered. You can't get welfare until you do the custody / maintenance thing in court. When I did the court thing with my crappy legal aid lawyer, who couldn't even remember my name, What's-His-Ass-Crack didn't even bother showing up. Maybe I didn't even have the right address for him; I'd pretty much lost track of him by then. The Right Honourable Legal Aid told me not to even bother asking for child support because no judge would order it because the sperm source was on welfare. I wore good pants and a shirt with little flowers and grey stripes that I'd borrowed from Em. I wanted to make a good impression. I wanted nothing bad to happen. Em waited in the hall for me while it was going on, and the whole thing was over before I realized it. I was terrified the whole time I was in the giant old law courts building. I could feel little bits of myself slipping away, chipping off and bouncing down the long hallways, and I couldn't do anything about it. Em gave me a hug and said, "Okay?" I nodded, and we walked back up Broadway and Balmoral, in and out of the shadows of the bloated elms and all those giant brick houses with porches and blank window-eyes. We treated the kids to grilled cheese sandwiches at The Nook, checked out the paperbacks at the Sally Ann, and then went home, my new official piece of paper tucked deep in the blue diaper bag. I made a photocopy of it at the camera place on Sherbrook, sent it off to the Social Assistance office with my case number written on the top, and that was it. They said Jump, I said Fine, whatever. The files on me that exist in various metal cabinets in this world got a millimetre thicker.

UWV Showdowns usually feature at least one screaming fit, and that's generally worth the price of admission. Neither Em nor I have TV channels, only old VCRs and pawnshop videos, so we consider this our very own Hallmark Hall of Shame Movie of the Week. Melodrama at its finest.

"Jeremy. How've you been?" Kristen's voice drifts over to us from where she's leaning in the window of a Ford Focus right in front of the building. She's wearing makeup, and a skirt that's probably a little short for leaning over like that.

"Her boyfriend dumped her. Again," Em says, digging in her diaper bag for Ali's sippy-cup. "I saw her at the library at story time. Dumped her youngest kid with the librarian and was sitting with the Seasonal books, crying her fucking eyes out." She shakes her head and laughs. "Pretty soon they're not going to even let any of us in the fucking library anymore."

"So what's with the skirt? And Christ, I don't think I've ever seen her in lipstick before. Do they even still make that colour? What is that, like Tangerine Dream or something? Sexual Revolution à l'Orange?"

We're bitches. It's true. But don't for a second think that the other women didn't talk about us the same way. Although they probably weren't as funny. At least, we thought we were funny. There just wasn't a whole lot else to do. And anyway, it was just talking. Last week, when I saw Kristen put a loaf of bread back at the corner store because she didn't have enough for bread and milk and oranges, I waited until she'd left and then bought an extra loaf and left it hanging in a plastic bag on her door. No big deal. It was just crappy Wonder Bread. No one else is really looking out for any of us. We don't necessarily do a great job of looking out for each other, but sometimes we try.

"Duh," Em says, rolling her eyes. "Every time that dirtbag dumps her, she decides she's going back to Jeremy. Except he's just a dirtbag with a better haircut. And anyway, she's too old for him now. He only likes the nineteen-year-old blondes with big tits." She pops a grape in her mouth. "Remember Lisette? Her cousin's a cleaner in Jeremy's office. Now there's a girl with big tits. Smart, though. She says he likes to Work Late. And then the next morning she's picking skanky red thongs out of the office plants."

"Classy," I say. That's Winnipeg, anyway. Somehow, everybody knows everybody else. It's a pretty tough city to try anonymity in. Doesn't matter what's going on in your life; the second you walk out the door, feeling good about yourself, you're pretty much guaranteed to run into someone who remembers your excruciatingly bad perm, circa 1989. Or the time you were trying to pee at a bush party and fell into the fire. No secrets, about your past, your present, or even your future.

"This should get good in a minute. Her Eau de Desperation must have pretty much wafted through his car by now. Look," she says, laughing. "He's starting to do that weird neck twitch thing."

Sure enough, Jeremy's head started ticking over to the right. He had his body twisted around, trying to reach the back door to open it for the kids, who were standing behind Kristen. Shanelle, the littlest one, was hanging onto Kristen's leg. Jade and Sari, the older two, stood with their arms crossed, looking off down the street, affecting that bored and world-weary posture that only preteen girls can really pull off.

"I just think it might be fun, Jeremy!" Kristen's voice was louder now, with an ugly sheen of shrill. "It used to be really fun!" Her voice drops an octave, but she can't shake the shrillness. "You remember, baby, how great it was? It could be, you know, really great." Jade and Sari look at each other, grab the back car door, yank it open, and clamber in. Shanelle's started to cry, and she's still got the Vulcan death grip on Kristen's leg. Kristen's kind of shaking her leg, and one hand has reached down to stroke Shanelle's head. Jeremy's got his head down on the steering wheel, his head still twitching.

"Whaddaya think?" I ask Em. "Tourette's?" This is another favourite game. Most of us have been diagnosed with something or other at various times in our lives. Often multiple, contradictory things. It's all crap, really. Doctors never get it right. You walk into a doctor's office, asking for actual testing for some actual thing that you've actually researched. And as soon as they hear you're a single mom, they get all paternalistic and stop listening. *No, no,* they say. *I'm sure your thyroid is fine. Why don't you just try these? Just three a day, like a good girl.* And then they hand you a sample box of Paxil or Zoloft or whatever new antidepressant their reps dropped off for them that day. And those are the good ones. Every now and then you meet a real asshole who says, *History of drug abuse? Hmm. Cry a lot, do you? Exactly how many piercings do you have?* And then they decide you're bipolar or psychotic or something, load you up on the serious crazy meds, sometimes try to get you into the hospital. When seriously, all you really needed was your goddamned thyroid checked.

And then, when you really do have something going on, they don't have the time of day for you, and they treat you like a pusher on a school corner when you ask for some Ativan or something. *We simply don't have the resources to deal with that,* they say. *I suggest you get your mom to help out more.* I generally suggest that they call my mom and run that by her, see what happens. Em just tells them that her mom is dead.

Sometimes trying to talk to Melanie was like trying to talk to those doctors. Like, we just spoke completely different languages. Or, more likely, I was the bilingual one and I just got fucking tired of translating. The day we broke up, Cal was hanging out downstairs at Em's, and Mel and I were sharing a smoke in my messy bed. The perfect Sunday afternoon light kissed the tips of my bare toes and lit up the faint freckles on her cheeks and the soft skin on her smooth, muscled shoulders. I felt an uncontrollable urge to lick them, and stubbed my smoke out so I could reach for her.

"Hang on," she'd said, pulling away from me to sit up against the pillows. "I want to talk to you."

"Oh yeah?" I'd said, following her across the bed, smiling into the damp skin at her neck. "I can think of a couple of things we can talk about."

"No, seriously, stop it," she'd said. "I seriously think we need to talk."

I'd closed my eyes against the softness of her throat for a minute, sighed, and moved away, bunched the pillows behind my back so I could lean against the wall. This sounded ominously similar to lots of other 'talks' we'd had, more and more lately.

"Listen, babe," she'd said. "I know you get mad when I say this."

"So don't fucking say it, then."

"See, that's what I mean. You're so defensive. I think it's just a coping mechanism, one that's not really helping you. I think you haven't really dealt with your past."

Oh good, I'd thought. The Dealt With My Past talk. My favourite. Right up there, in the general scheme of things, with the I'm Sorry, It's Too Late For An Epidural talk. Or the We Mailed Your Cheque Two Weeks Ago, If You Haven't Received It Yet It Will Take Another Two Weeks To Process

A New One talk.

"I was talking to my therapist about it, and she said that —"

"Don't talk to your therapist about me, Mel, for fuck's sake. I'm sure she's a super lady and that her deep spiritual inner life and weekend Reiki seminar in Hawaii totally qualifies her to, like, accurately diagnose my Deep Trauma and Wounded Inner Child, but seriously, just don't."

"See, that's exactly what I mean," Mel had said. "You're doing it again. Everything's a fucking joke, a smartass comment. Do you realize that you've never cried in front of me? Never? That even when you're talking about horrible, horrible things, rape and abuse and addiction and sitting on some street corner asking people for money, you've never cried? You've never really been, truly, vulnerable. You talk about it like it's no big deal. I just don't think you've ever really faced it, ever really worked through it. Baby, I can't even imagine how much it hurts you, inside. Just let me in. I promise, I promise I'll hold you, all the way through."

I'd looked over at Mel, who'd had tears in her own eyes by this point. And I'd just felt tired. And kind of like a lab rat in an observation maze. And Mel was the giant scientist in the white coat with the clipboard. And the orange blob of cheese just wasn't much incentive anymore. I'd pulled a T-shirt over my head and lit another smoke.

"Okay, Melanie," I'd said. "I know you mean well. Honest, I know you're speaking from a place of love and good vibes and whatever. I'm sorry, I'm not trying to be a jerk. It's just, I have cried. A lot, okay? I just don't really need to do that every day. Or with you. It's not more real if I cry, you know? I'm not an abandoned puppy you picked up on a street corner somewhere. You don't have to take me home and feed me." Her eyes had still looked watery, but also pissed off. And, I don't know, greedy. Hungry for a little piece of vicarious darkness, something she could hold and polish up and show her friends. *So, my lover told me that when she used to cook up heroin....* Dirty.

We'd sat around for the rest of the afternoon and talked and talked and talked like good little lesbians, but I'd known it was pointless. She didn't get it, I couldn't figure out how to explain it. Done. She'd eventually left, and I'd stomped down to Em's to pick up Cal.

"What's up?" Em had asked. "You look bitchy."

"I broke up with Mel," I'd said, rummaging through Em's cupboards. "Do you have any crackers? I'm totally craving salt."

"Behind the Krap Dinner," she'd said, waving her hand vaguely over her shoulder in the direction of the cupboard above the fridge. "What happened?"

I'd found the soda crackers, and was trying to tear open the plastic with my teeth. "She wanted me to bleed on her."

"Ah," Em had nodded. "Sublimated Florence Nightingale desire trajectory, coupled with homoerotic expressions of her own deep-seated pathological lack of self-esteem. Plus, too many undergrad Women's Studies classes."

"Fucking lesbians," I'd said through a mouthful of crackers.

"Well, you're the one who keeps fucking them," Em had laughed. She'd hugged me, hard, kissed the top of my head, and then started hunting around for the kids' jackets. "Come on, baby-dyke," she'd said. "I know what'll make you feel better. Let's get the kids together and go walk up and down in front of the creepy Christian cult house in the Gates. We'll hold hands and sing Indigo Girls songs and totally freak them out while they're having Bible study or Beat Your Children hour or whatever. I totally think we should get a bunch of welfare moms together and buy the house across the street from them."

"And have a big statue of Ganesh on the lawn, and biker chick parties every Friday, and feminist performance art exhibitions every Saturday afternoon," I'd said, smiling. We'd played this game before, a lot. It was a good one. It generally got us through.

Jeremy's still sitting in the car, twitching his neck. Kristen's still hanging in the car window, her words drifting in and out of earshot. Em squints her eyes to get a better look.

"Nah. Not Tourette's," she says thoughtfully. "I've seen him other places. He only tics around Kristen."

"Oppositional Defiance Disorder? Look at the way he won't even look at her."

"That one's bullshit. That's just something school psychologists made up for when kids don't do exactly what they say when they say it." She pops another grape in her mouth and chews for a minute. I glance over at the kids — her girl Ali, and my boy Cal. They're behind the plastic yellow Tic-Tac-Toe tiles, planting twigs from the molting bushes in the sand.

"I've got it!" she says triumphantly, and twists her body around on the bench to get a better look. "APD. Antisocial Personality Disorder. In other words, a high-functioning sociopath. In other words, your everyday, run-of-the-mill prick with no conscience and no morals."

"Good one," I say. Jeremy's now revving the car engine like a NASCAR driver. Kristen's still gripping the driver's window, which he's trying to roll up. Jade's already gotten out of the car, pried Shanelle off Kristen's leg, and is strapping her in the backseat, yelling at her dad not to drive away yet because the door's still open. Kristen's given up on seduction, and is safely back in the Land of Rage.

"You bastard!" she's yelling. "You fucking prick! You fucking... sociopath!"

"High five for Kristen," I mutter.

"Where's my fucking child support cheque?!" she yells. "If I have to call Maintenance again, so help me god —"

"C'mon," Em says, stuffing things into her diaper bag. "I'm bored. Let's go in."

"But it's just getting good," I say.

"Whatever. Tune in next week, folks, for episode four million and twelve. Besides, I rented *The Land Before Time*. That should keep the kids occupied for a couple of hours."

"I hate those fucking dinosaurs," I say. "Especially that little prissy one. It's like, cartoons to slit your throat by." But I gather up my stuff and my kid, and troop behind Em and Ali into the building. With most of the kids gone, weekends are pretty quiet around here. The next big excitement will be

Sunday night, when the Daddy cars line up on the street again, disgorging grimy, hyperactive kids back to their moms, the kids all clutching crappy McDonald's toys.

Occasionally there are whole families living in the building. Immigrants, mostly. Probably refugees. Moms and dads and kids. They don't tend to stay long. As soon as they figure out what's what, they move on to something better. I still have the phone number for that place on Ruby tucked away in my pocket. Melanie had really wanted me to get out of this building. She kept saying that I was better than this. I wasn't sure what she really meant by that, and it kind of pissed me off. When I saw the ad with the little paper tags on the bottom I imagined her voice in my head, just for a minute. I imagined her in some new space with me, talking on the phone. *Yeah,* she'd say. *I'm just at my girlfriend's place right now. Really close by, just over on Ruby.* And she'd look at me and smile and reach out and rest her hand on my thigh. There'd be leafy trees outside the window, and the bright sticky sunlight would twist through the green and splash our entire bodies. And in that tiny moment of shadow and yellow light and her open face turned toward me, there would just be love, swollen and sweet. Just that.

In reality, I probably can't afford the place. I mean, when you only get like $850 a month from welfare, it's tough to spend almost $500 on rent. And then you have to factor in utilities. There's a couple of rent subsidy programs, but they're hardly anything and besides, you're only eligible if you're working, not collecting. And if you're working, you also have to figure in daycare costs — if you can even find a subsidized spot at some place that's not a secret child sweat-shop or something. Em and I have gone over and over it. Working minimum wage, paying daycare and real rent some-where, plus all the transportation, you're actually not really much better off than staying here on assistance. It's a differ-ence of like a hundred bucks a month or something, once you figure it all out. It's a bit better on student loans. Em and I periodically drift in and out of university. The subsidized rent is even cheaper if you're a student, and it's a little easier to work out daycare. But what the fuck am I going to universi-ty for? It's not like I'm going to be an architect or a dentist or something. My incomplete Arts degree has given me some truly excellent vocabulary and a smartass trick of naming the systems of power and exploitation that apparently got me here and keep me stuck. Capitalism, patriarchy, hegemonic heteronormative blah blah blah. But it doesn't really help me get out. And one day they expect you to pay those loans back.

I decide to pass on the dinosaur movie, and Cal and I take the elevator up to our second-floor apartment. All the apart-ments are basically the same. Off-white walls that you're not allowed to paint and that are pretty much guaranteed never to look exactly clean. Two or three bedrooms, depending on how many kids you have. A little kitchen space that's more like a hallway than an actual room. They're okay. Bigger, really, than what you'd get in the real world. I've really tried, but it's just hard to make them look anything other than anonymous, transient. I have a couple of plants that I usually forget to water. I found a bag of beautiful old embroidered tablecloths at a garage sale, and I draped them over milk crates stacked up on either side of the couch, as well as on the kitchen table; I change the one on the table every Monday morning. One week birds, the next sailboats with roses, and then the cartoon-like cactuses. Something beautiful, just for me and Cal. Something that moves us through the weeks. I've got Waterhouse pictures on the walls, and mismatched furniture that I've scavenged from Wolseley, just across Sherbrook, a neighbourhood of philosophy profs and socially-conscious lawyers and giant houses painted yellow and blue with yards full of eco-friendly flowers and feng-shui genuine Tibetan wind chimes.

Sometimes Em works over in Wolseley, under the table, odd and ends stuff. Walking dogs. Emergency babysitting. She says it's mostly rich people vacillating between guilt and self-righteousness, people who read *The Utne Reader*, hire single moms like her, and think they're Down With the People. People who read *The Summer of My Amazing Luck*, and say things to her like, *I think you're just so brave to walk into a welfare office. I could never do that.*

You can do just about anything in this world, really, and not even think much about it. Just another day with a hungry kid and no bus fare. You can even get good at it.

The phone rings. Cal's playing in his room with plastic farm animals. I pick up the phone, and it's Em.

"Hey, do you have any tampons?" she asks. "I forgot to pick some up at Shopper's earlier."

"Uh huh," I say. "Just give me a sec. I'll run some down to you."

I hang up and walk into the bathroom, start rummaging around under the cupboard. Toilet paper, hooded bath towels with dinosaurs on them. Empty toothpaste box. Plastic bath ducks. Behind that, dust balls. An earring I thought I'd lost a couple of months ago. Hair elastics. Scissors. A stray coupon for Melba toast (expired), which I'm obviously never going to use. No fucking tampons. I check my bedroom — the closet, under the bed, behind the dresser — and the storage closet and even the bottom kitchen cupboards. Still no tampons.

I stomp into the living room and dial the phone. Em picks up on the third ring.

"She took my fucking tampons!" I yell into the phone.

"What?" says Em. "What did you do with your tampons? Why are you yelling?"

"I didn't do anything with my goddamned tampons. Melanie must've taken them. It's the only explanation, goddammit."

Em just laughs. "That's what happens when you date girls," she says archly. I kind of miss Mel. Okay, I miss her a lot, sometimes. She honestly believed that she loved me, but really, all she wanted was to be the big strong woman who kissed it all better, who was magnanimous enough to overlook my indiscretions. Except they weren't indiscretions. They were just stuff that I did. Or stuff that happened. When you're in the middle of it, it's just the way it is. And everyone else was in the middle of it too, at the time. It's not like I was the only one. It's not like that stuff had any currency. So what if I always told them as funny stories? Who was she to decide that I wasn't Dealing With It? The thing is, some of the stories really were funny. And the funnier they were, the more they broke your heart. Em and I broke each other's hearts, every day. All the women in the building did. If we sat around and told our sad, sad stories every day, we'd flood the whole damn building with tears. So we laughed instead, and raged, and yelled, and cracked jokes. We left bread on each other's door knobs and watched out for all the kids when their own moms couldn't and diagnosed each other with crazy disorders and plotted escape. And if you really knew how to listen, you'd get it.

"Whatever," Em says into the phone. "I got tired of waiting for you, so I went and knocked on Kristen's door."

"Oh god," I said. "How is she, poor cow?"

"She's fine, actually. We were bad girls, and had a couple shots of tequila. Hey, did you know she spent a summer at Wreck Beach too? Like, the same summer Steve and I were there. Weird, eh?"

"But you never noticed her because you were too busy picking sand out of your crack?" I offered, lighting a cigarette and settling into the corner of the couch for a good chat.

Robyn forbade us to wear black so I wear grey and pink. Marie didn't know and she shows up in an elegant black suit with tails and a stiff collar, white shirt and black tie; it is so outrageous that it is acceptable after all. We all get there really early and stand outside, smoking cigarettes and reviewing the rules. No black. Sit as close to the front as possible. Maintain eye contact. Bring vodka. No crying. We don't see Robyn, but when people start to arrive we go inside, through the foyer panelled in dark wood. We stand in line and sign the guest book, like it's a wedding or a house warming. What do you say? We would write something courageous and witty but we know her mom will read it and maybe be offended and certainly take it out on Robyn, so we each write in small black letters, *So sorry* and, *With greatest sympathy*. The four of us sit in the middle of a long pew behind the aunts and uncles. We are a different kind of family. The room fills up behind us, standing room only. We talk about what we'd want. Drag queens. Tumblers. Fire-eaters. Flashing lights. Open bar. Ellen says she'd want nothing at all and we all stop talking. Marie picks at her cufflinks. Lise checks her watch, and I wonder if there is a real organ somewhere, Phantom of the Funeral Home, or if it's all pre-recorded. Is there a CD marketed specifically to directors for these occasions? Music to Mourn By: All Time Greatest Hits.

How do you know what size of room to book? How did Robyn sit through the arithmetic of adding up a family, a career, golf friends and drinking buddies, people she knew, people she'd never met, people she didn't know about? Add. Multiply. Estimate. A room too big looks cavernous, pathetic. A room too small is crowded, hot, uncomfortable. Like a concert promoter choosing a venue, banking on reputation. And you always wonder, the small mean question: how many at mine? How many do I add up to?

Robyn's ex-girlfriend and her new partner show up, take seats at the back of the room. Ellen spotted them coming through the doors and we can't believe their audacity. Christina cheated on Robyn with Erin and now they're both here, for what? Sorry I broke your heart, and oh yeah, so sorry for your loss? Plus they're wearing black, both of them. We make a plan to keep them away from Robyn, team effort.

The family files in. Robyn scans the room, looking for us. We sit up straight, the wood hard against our backs. I have the urge to raise my hand and wave at her, yes, yes, we're here. I resist and she finally spots us, right up front, just like she asked. We nod and smile small and she smiles back and I think, How are we all smiling? This is ridiculous, none of us should be here, we should be back at the bar, drinking in the middle of the day, watching traffic through slats in the blinds, playing Macy Gray and deciding the DJ lineup for the month, being silly and efficient until Robyn goes back to the hospital. This feels like a dress rehearsal for a play I never want to see, the floor marked, lines counted off and stiff, everyone uncomfortable in their costumes.

It begins. We wait for Robyn's eulogy. I don't think she should be the one to give it but her mother can't and her brother won't. Finally she gets up and walks to the podium and Marie surreptitiously hands a package of Kleenex to each of us even though we're not supposed to cry, but just in case. Robyn is a perfectly composed wreck. She's been living on gin for weeks and her steps are steady but I can see her hands shake. None of us know what she is going to say; she said she could only say it once, here, today. There's a long pause and I think she's not going to make it and then she takes a deep breath and says, *At twenty-one, I'm not supposed to lose my dad. He's not supposed to die. This is not supposed to happen.* Lise's eyes get glassy and she has to look down, fumbling for the Kleenex. I stare straight ahead at Robyn and think: trees, rock, implacable, fortitude, dignity, iron, and I'm sure she can hear me. The room cries quietly around me, and Robyn and I lock gazes, or at least I think we do. Maybe she's not seeing anything, anybody. Maybe all she hears is her own voice, her own heart beating crazily inside some achingly empty chamber. It's a beautiful speech, sad and loving and feral around the edges. A friend of her dad's speaks too and I think, This is a man I never really knew. Now he does not exist and this whole room is trying to grab hold of a piece of something that's gone and hang on, hang on, and Robyn is hanging on admirably, holding her girlfriend Sam's hand while Sam weeps, and I don't know what to feel.

The minister gets up to talk. She didn't really know Robyn's dad, but a minister always seems to be called for in these situations. She talks about her own father, how he is a salesman and a carpenter. Of course, he is still alive, so I'm not sure what she is trying to say. And then she calls Robyn's dad Calvin. Calvin is her uncle, sitting to Robyn's left beside her Aunt Marion. She calls him Calvin again, and the room rustles. We have become one entity, all these people crowded together in the room; we have united against this minister. *What a fucking moron*, mumbles Ellen, and I hold her hand to keep her from standing up. *Let us*, says the minister, *remember Calvin*, and we have become a congregation, we are outraged, and in one voice we all say, *Carlo*. Let us remember Carlo. Let this stupid woman learn his name before the service begins, let us not make this Tuesday afternoon even more weird and outrageous and unreal than it already is, let us not heap travesty on top of tragedy. She turns a suitable shade of mortified red, she apologizes; the service inches along. I stare at the picture of Robyn's dad, Carlo; he is handsome and smiling under his moustache. He looks like Tom Selleck. Beside the picture is the urn, and the minister is finally, thankfully, finished.

Music starts playing again, Sarah McLachlan. Something heartbreaking that pulsates and throbs. Which of her songs couldn't you play at a funeral? Robyn's mom is weeping and Robyn has to lead her from the room. I decide that at my funeral I want disco, something strobing and flashing. I will never ask Robyn to give my eulogy; once in her lifetime is enough.

The reception is upstairs; the family is there already. Is it a reception, or is that only for weddings? I am so ignorant, but Lise and Ellen and Marie don't know either. There will be small sandwiches and coffee. The family will stand in an excruciating line and shake everyone's hand, and when we get up there we will slip Robyn a Perrier bottle full of straight vodka because we promised we would. Standing in the foyer we see Christina and Erin and suddenly we have a purpose. Ellen and Marie stand beside the stairs, ready to block them if they try to go up. I go talk to them, and Lise stands behind me with her arms folded across her chest. I am angry enough to stop a small army of adulterous ex-girlfriends. I'm not sure what I say, but I'm talking low with my arms flying around my body and Lise is laughing and Christina and Erin leave and I don't care if they hold it against me forever. Robyn never knows that they were there.

Upstairs we hand off the Perrier-vodka to Robyn as we shake the hands of all these strangers that are her family. Sam weeps and holds on to Lise's neck long enough to hold up the line. There is a small awkward moment when Robyn's mom announces that she'd like some Perrier too, and the funeral director tells her that they have none and she gives Robyn a long, knowing, suspicious look. Robyn slips outside for a cigarette with us and we're all afraid to touch each other, fragile and serene and ready to shatter as she is, stupid and stumbling as we are. We smoke silently, leaning against the warm brick wall in the alley at the side of the building. She says, *Thank you guys for coming, so much*. We all jump in, *Of course, of course*. She says, *Thank you for not wearing black*. Marie says, *I didn't know, I'm sorry*. Robyn puts her hand on her shoulder, says, *Are you kidding? You look great. Thank you for the Perrier*. And we laugh a little. *Thank you for not crying. I needed you not to. That was so hard*. I'm full of pride and exhaustion and helplessness. Ellen lights another cigarette off the dying one in her hand. Robyn takes a slow swallow of vodka. The afternoon sun leans onto our shoulders, long and hot and indifferent. I wait for Robyn to cry, I have been waiting for weeks. She doesn't cry. She smoothes the front of her shirt, touches her left earring, turns and walks back into the funeral home. The four of us watch her disappearing into the darkness, blinking back the sun.

"And then after it's all connected, you just push the round button, here," I said. Gran sat beside me at her shiny dining room table, in the little alcove that Grandpa built onto the house forty years ago. He and Gran's brother Peter had decided on parquet flooring for the little room, and spent days and days longer than they'd planned nailing tiny strips of wood into the floor, the nails invisible when they were finished. He always wanted to give Gran good things, nice things, things that would last. They couldn't afford to buy them, so he just hauled out his tools and made them. I couldn't do anything like that. Grandpa was gone, but his hands were all over this little house in St. Boniface, down the street from Canada Packers. When I was a kid and we'd come to visit, the air felt thick and yellow; the smoke from the meat-packing plant seeped through the streets, under doorways, wrapping around tree trunks and leaves, the stench sitting cloudy in your lungs, a viscous coating inside your nose and throat. *I can't breathe*, I'd think. *How do people live here?* And then after a few hours you didn't even notice it anymore and all I could smell was Gran's particular house smell: lemon floor cleaner and wood wax, rose spray in the bathroom, an echo of slightly burnt roast beef in the kitchen, a faint must rising up from the basement.

Gran had put placemats under my old computer to protect the wood of her table, thick woven mustard-coloured cloth that she probably bought at The Bay a million years ago, hemmed herself on the old beige sewing machine downstairs. I rested my left hand on the scratchy cloth, pressed the pads of my fingers into the fibres, willing microscopic flakes of skin to detach from my body, tangle into the coarse threads.

"It's just amazing, really," Gran said, watching the boot-up menu on the black computer screen. "Really," she said again, shaking her head. "We didn't even have a telephone on the farm for years." I'd unplugged her kitchen phone, the one with the long gnarled beige cord that you could stretch around the corner if you wanted a semblance of privacy, and plugged in my modem cord.

"This is email," I said, and clicked open my inbox. It was kind of dumb, really, to haul my whole computer to my grandmother's house, along with a hockey bag full of clothes, a backpack of books, and my shitty green acoustic guitar. And, of course, my baby, Gwen, and all of her stuff: diapers, crackers, toys, stroller, blankets, stuffed Eeyore, baby first aid kit, whatever. Gran had most of that stuff around her house anyway, salvaged from her own kids, cast off and tucked away from various grandkids over the years. But I thought Gwennie might feel better with her own things, might pick up on a kind of stability or security from being wrapped in her very own blanket, despite being in a strange bed, despite the tremor in my fingers as I tucked the soft blue hem around her shoulders as she finally fell asleep. And I thought Gran would like the computer, would like to see how it worked.

That wasn't entirely true. Of course Gran liked the computer, and was eager for me to show her how to turn it on, how to surf the web. She was determined to embrace the world as much as possible. While she still had time, she said. She'd bought a huge map of the world, and unfolded it on her kitchen table whenever she watched the news on the little kitchen TV Grandpa had mounted under the shelves for her before he'd died. She said that so many countries had changed names and shapes since she was in school that she didn't always know what they were talking about on The National. She'd watch Peter Mansbridge and trace her fingers through Africa, Eastern Europe, sketching borders with her thumbnail. And she'd talk back at the TV when something made her mad. "Foolishness," she'd snap, shaking her head. Just the way she used to snap at Grandpa. "Oh, that man!" she'd say to no one in particular. And Grandpa would grin and wink at me behind her back, carry on with whatever he was doing that made her mad in the first place — stealing bits of carrots out of the saucepan with his fingers, peeling an onion to eat whole like an apple, clicking his dentures around in his mouth.

And so I knew that Gran would like the computer, wouldn't even mind it sprawled across her good table. And there wasn't much else I could offer her. I was the one who had called in the middle of the night, and she'd come to pick us up in her old maroon sedan, no questions asked. I didn't tell her what was going on, and she didn't ask, just popped the trunk of her car, helped me shove stuff in, and then reached through the back passenger door on the other side to help me figure out how to attach the car seat for Gwen. She asked lots of questions, in general, but she was very good at not asking questions that I didn't really want to answer. Personal questions. I didn't have any money, and I couldn't really chip in for groceries or anything. So I brought the computer, and the guitar, and I thought, maybe I can play her some songs. Teach her about technology.

But really, the thought of not bringing the stupid computer terrified me. I didn't sleep much at night anymore, just sort of napped off and on with Gwennie through the whole twenty-four hour clock. We were both night owls, and it was a good schedule for us, but it made me feel kind of crazy, too. Our timetable didn't work the same as the rest of the world. We'd be waking up just as stores were closing, bored and lonely at three in the morning when everyone else was sleeping. Sometimes it felt like we lived in a plastic hamster ball, rolling through the world but not able to actually touch anything or anyone, not able to actually communicate or interact with anyone else. Only each other. I hugged her wispy little head close under my chin, breathed in her warm, milky powder baby smell, and felt my heart crack and slip inside me.

Apart from Gwennie, the best thing I'd gotten out of my relationship with Greg was learning how to use the Internet. He'd be out at night, usually — a friend's place, some bar, whatever — and I'd log on, Gwennie on my lap. He'd shown me a chat program, and I'd figured out how to actually use it. And I'd started to connect with people. Women, mostly. From all over the world. "It's always noon somewhere," my high school friend Michelle used to say when she poured herself a glass of cheap white wine with breakfast. It was always evening somewhere too, even when it was black outside my own window and I couldn't call any of my real friends because they were sleeping. At first I was just blown away that I was actually talking — typing — in real time to some woman that I didn't even know in Australia or New Zealand or somewhere, and I didn't even really know what to say. But somehow the anonymous typing made it easier to say the things that I really did want to say. The things that I needed to say, the things that were just too damn hard to actually say out loud, looking right into a real person's eyes. Waiting for the fallen face, the tightened lips, the thing at the edges of the eyes that looked like pity or contempt or secret relief at being spared, untouched, themselves.

It was scary to type all that stuff, to put it all into words and sentences and send it off with held breath and open throat into the world, because I knew that Greg could come home at any minute. That had happened a couple of times, and I'd just hit the power button on the extension cord with my toe, just turned the whole machine off mid-sentence. And then when he'd pass out I'd sneak back out to the living room, log on again and let those faceless women know that I was okay. Lots of them would be waiting for me, to make sure. Or they'd left messages with other women still online: *Tell Lem to email me.* Lem was my screen name; it was just my own name backwards, and I'd told most of them my real name anyway, but I liked having another name. It almost made me feel like I could have another self, a better self tucked away inside me waiting for the right time to come out. There was the real me, Mel, broke, confused, scared, running away from my boyfriend with my baby, sitting at my grandmother's dining room table, hating myself for feeling like I'd put her in danger, jumping every time I heard something on the quiet street, sure that it was Greg, that he'd figured out where we were, that he'd come after us. And then there was the other real me, Lem, always quick with a funny comeback, insightful, brave, resilient, articulate. Loved.

"Where's this from?" Gran asked, pointing to the top email.

"Israel," I said. "She's in Tel Aviv. Her name's Rakia. She sent that little black motorcycle jacket for Gwen."

"Isn't that something," Gran said. "Grandpa and I never went to Israel. I would've liked to have seen the Dead Sea." Gran and Grandpa had taken up square dancing after their kids had grown up and they'd both retired, first Grandpa from the packing plant, then a couple of years later Gran from the customer service counter at The Bay. Square dancing and golfing. They'd travelled a lot with their square dancing group, all over the States and Europe, and there was a whole shoebox full of pictures. There were way more women in the group than men, and they jokingly called it Hank's Harem, my grandpa standing and smiling in the middle of the group shots, a line of white and grey haired women stretching out from either arm, all of them in matching yellow and orange satin western costumes. There were some other men, too, hair neatly slicked back, silver bolero ties dangling from under pointed collars. And the caller was always a man, too, of course. But it was still Hank's Harem.

Most of their traveling photographs were pretty boring. Churches and cathedrals. Group shots on the steps of important buildings, or lining up in front of the buses. Lots of scenery pictures with no people in them. But there were a couple that I really loved, that I dug out every time I went over. One was from the early 70s; Gran had a stiff bouffant hairdo and an avocado coloured coat. Her body stood a little sideways, and she'd turned her head to look right at the camera, a huge smile lifting up her whole face. And peeking out over the top of her head was a little grey monkey, sitting right on her shoulders, one little hand resting on top of her hair, its big-eyed wrinkled monkey face looking straight at me. In the picture, one of Gran's hands was blurred and reaching up to her head, as if to pull the monkey off, or catch it in case it fell. I'm not sure which. I don't know where it was taken. Gibraltar, maybe. That monkey is surely dead now. But there's something so alive about the picture, both of them taken by surprise by the flash of the camera, that little tiny second in time recorded forever, sitting in a shoebox, waiting for a granddaughter to pull it out, wondering about places where wiry furred creatures could just jump at you out of nowhere and you wouldn't even be afraid, just smile in amazement.

"What's that one?" Gran asked, pointing at another email. I squinted at the screen.

"Oh fuck," I said. "Shit. Oh, god, sorry Gran. It's nothing. Sorry. Don't worry about it." I reached for the mouse, clicked to minimize the screen. I didn't want to read an email from Greg, especially one whose subject line read *You can't hide forever*. I didn't want Gran reading it. I didn't want her to worry. *Selfish bitch,* I told myself. How could I have come here? How could I have thought that this was a safe place to hide out for a while? Greg knew where this house was; he'd been here for Christmases, Easter dinners. I just hoped that he wouldn't put it together and figure out that Gwen and I were actually here. I hoped he'd think that we'd skipped town, or that we'd gone to my mom's or something, maybe even a shelter, anywhere but here. I mean, really, who'd be stupid enough to decide that the home of a tiny eighty-year-old woman was the best place to hide from a violent, probably drunk, and certainly pissed-off boyfriend?

Apart from me, of course. My stomach felt bottomless and black and my heart dropped straight down into it like a brick. The muscles in my shoulders were trembling jelly, and the backs of my eyes burned. I'd left, hadn't I? I'd told Greg it was done, and gotten a locksmith to come out and change the locks on the doors. Not before Greg had thrown a few closing punches, but after he'd stormed out. I'd done the smart thing, the healthy thing, the right thing. All the women online had been so happy for me, though some had been scared. Marla had even offered me and Gwen a ticket to Sydney, but I couldn't accept that. It was too much to actually take, but just the fact that she'd offered shifted something inside me, snapped open a piece of ice to let something warm seep through.

And I was happy. I really was. I was glad, I was happy, I was finally finally free. I just couldn't understand why I was also so terrified.

Gran was watching me, her lips tight. "I'm going to bed," she said. "Tomorrow you can show me a web site. Stay up as long as you want. You won't disturb me." She stood up from the table, lifted her chair back over the flooring so it wouldn't scratch, and walked toward her bedroom, the one at the front with the white curtains. Just a couple of years before Grandpa died, they'd finally replaced their two twin beds, side by side, with a double bed with a brass frame. Grandpa's dresser still stood on his side of the bed, the porcelain dog face that still held his glasses standing sentinel on top of the white doily. Grandpa had a bad back, and his twin bed had had a sheet of wood slipped under the mattress to make it firmer, but they'd usually slept together in Gran's little twin bed anyway. I guess there's always as much room as you believe there is. I wondered if Gran liked all the extra space alone in her double bed, or if she was lonely at night. She never really said.

She paused at the corner to her bedroom, turned and looked back at me. "If your grandpa was still alive," she said, "he'd get out his shotgun." I didn't say anything, and she turned and walked around the corner.

I sat, stuck to the chair, and listened to her bedroom door click closed, listened to the muffled hum of the news as she switched on the bedroom TV set. I felt tiny, tiny as the sharp end of a pin, small as one white fleck of salt in the shaker shoved off to the side of the table. The room swelled up around my small body, the walls looming, the decorative china plates painted with pictures of dogs and kittens round and swollen and bloated, the glass in the china hutch rattling. And then it all fell away into nothingness, and I was alone for miles and miles in every direction, in the nuclear devastation of my own blown-out heart.

Greg was never going to build me a parquet floor. He was never going to get together with my brother and draw plans for anything, he was never going to get some job that he wasn't thrilled about but that paid okay so we could save up and buy a little house on some quiet street with kids playing on the sidewalks. We were never going to take up some lame hobby that our kids laughed at but we secretly thought was fun, and travel around the world together in our dotage.

I knew this. I knew all this. That's why I left. I knew that all he did was hang out with whoever, fuck around on the computer, drink too much, yell stupid things at me, forget to change the baby, spend money we didn't have. Sometimes take a swing. It didn't take a genius to see how it was.

But there's always room for something in your heart if you believe in it enough, and I'd believed in hope, in redemption. I believed in the tremors in his voice, late at night, when he told me about the kind of life he wanted for us, for me and him and Gwennie. I'd left, but really I'd been waiting. Waiting for him to see me, really see me, now that I was gone. Waiting for him to be sorry, really sorry, so sorry that it would all be different.

But he was never going to hide the nails deep inside the wood just so that I didn't catch my slippers, just because it was the right way to do it.

Grandpa probably wouldn't have taken out his shotgun. It probably would have been more like the times when we were kids, when a bunch of the grandkids were over and we were fooling around and pushed Gran over the edge a little. "Now look here!" she'd yell. "Does Grandpa have to take off his belt?" None of us had ever been hit with a belt, and the thought of it struck terror deep into our tiny sticky hearts. But Grandpa was the one who'd looked most scared at the thought that Gran might really be mad enough to make him do it.

Gran never would have put up with any of this, I realized. And Grandpa would never, never have done the stuff that Greg did. Probably partly because Gran put the fear of God in him. But mostly, and most importantly, because he loved her. And that's not what love did. Greg really was sorry, every time he fucked up. I believed that was true. It just wasn't enough any more.

The dining room walls came back into focus. Gwennie woke up and started to cry in the back bedroom, cutting through the rumble of Gran's TV leaking under the door of her bedroom and the white noise of my computer humming in front of me. I walked to the back and scooped Gwennie up, her black hair damp and moist, her eyes scrunched, her forehead grumpy and wrinkled and pink. I brought her back to the dining room, and sat down in front of the computer monitor, pulled my sweater up on the side to nurse her while I read my emails. I deleted Greg's without even looking at it, and clicked open the one from Rakia.

Lemling,

I sent off a money order today for fifty dollars Canadian. I know you didn't ask for it. If I'd asked you would have said no, so I just sent it. Deal.

Will you be online later? I'll look for you, and then I have to go to a boring art show. *yawn*

Be strong, darling girl. Be good to your grandmother. Be good to your little girl. Be good to yourself. Sending much love from far away.

MWAH

I smiled and something acrid leaked out of me, something that used to look a little bit like the tattered shreds of hope. And the holes left by those last little hopeful threads burned as something else slipped in, something cold and sharp like long silver needles. Fear. This little Tremblay house was sturdy and solid with love, with years of love and care knotted into its floors and walls and placemats like thousands of tightly linked and tangled hands, holding on. But it wasn't impenetrable, and the thick patina of love would not protect Gran or Gwennie from even one small act of rage or violence if Greg showed up.

And I understood now that of course he would, sooner or later. The love that clung to an old woman, a tiny baby, and one fucked-up girl would be nothing but cobwebs to him. He could be standing on the sloping front lawn right now, watching the light through all the windows, twisting his neck from side to side, watching the street for cars. His feet could be tensed in Gran's tiger lily patch under Gwennie's window, the soft fiery petals twisted and flat and unnoticed beneath him. I'd never know, until it was too late. The silver needles in my belly twisted and slammed their sharp metal tongues right through the stupid selfish bubble of safety that had been expanding inside me since Gran had picked me up and driven me here. Shame pooled, thick and black, between the recesses of my organs, inside my fingers, in the folds of my throat.

I reread Rakia's words. *Be strong, darling girl. Be good to your grandmother. Be good to your little girl. Be good to yourself.* I was an idiot. It was time for me to do what love did. It was time, past time, for me to truly be good to Gran, to Gwennie. And to myself.

I disconnected the modem, plugged the phone back in. I held the plastic receiver tightly to my ear, filled my lungs until they were swollen and bursting, and then released all the air, as steadily as I could manage. I dialed the number I'd learned by heart, my index finger wedged in the little hole in the rotary phone, the skin of my fingertip sliding around the dial, steadied by all the traces of my grandparents, my father, my aunts and uncles, my cousins, all the other fingers that had ever dialed this phone.

"You're going to be fine, honey," the woman on the other end of the phone said. "We'll send a cab for you now. Watch for it, okay?"

I shoved all my stuff, all Gwennie's stuff, into the black hockey bag. I was probably forgetting lots of things, clothes and toys and books I'd left scattered around the house, but it didn't really matter. Gran would gather it all up, keep it safe for me. I scribbled a quick note for Gran, explaining, and left it on the computer keyboard. I left the computer for her, running, humming on the table; she'd figure it out, or get a neighbour to help her. She'd like that. It would be another thing she'd keep safe for me. It was something tangible I could leave for her, something to say, *I'm sorry*, something to say, *Thank you*. Something to say, *I love you*.

I took a deep breath, lemon and rose, and pulled a chair over to the front window, tucked into the gold curtains at the side. I wrapped my feet around the legs of the chair, and shifted Gwennie's chubby heft in my arm, tighter against my body, and she nestled into me. Up the street, the black smoke billowed out from the tall chimney of the plant, nearly indistinguishable from the night sky. I heard Gran start to snore, a faint rattle, the quiet shiftings of an old woman in bed for the night. I watched for headlights sliding through the shadows of the street.

SUICIDE BOMBERS

I tried not to catch the eyes of the kids, even as they gathered around me, jostling, waiting with me for the ten-year-old crossing guard in her orange vest to step sideways off the curb, arm extended stiffly out to the right, left arm circling. She wore a blue nylon jacket that hung in loose bunches off her arms, and her rubber boots had kittens on them. Across the street was the school, old, white, slightly gothic, with wide stone steps climbing in tiny shallow increments up to the dark wooden front doors, the circle of dull and dirty stained glass serenely anchored in the middle of the building.

I would have been the child that noticed the blue and red glass. I would have been the child that stood on the front lawn every day at nine in the morning and again after lunch, staring at the promise of beauty. I would have stood very still, my eyes as open and unblinking as I could will them, the spaces between my ribs slipping open, the membranes of my small veins thinning, the pores of my skin sighing in release, opening my body up, dissolving the barriers between my small tightly wound self and this towering, rambling artifact, this covenant of dead hands to me, the one who could see it.

Or maybe not. Maybe I would have been entirely occupied by homework and the spelling test and how to finally get out of my turn at turning the rope and spend the whole glorious recess jumping, jumping, while the other girls chanted. Maybe I would have been so present in my own small life that

I never even noticed the sharp splinters of blue glass until it was too late, until the doors of the school were opened only to other children, smaller children, and I suddenly found myself locked out, locked up in the prologue of a girlhood that I hadn't expected and didn't entirely want. I wanted to be the one who knew what my hands held when they were cupped, rather than learning the shape and ache of regret later when my fingers were empty.

I wanted my fingers to stop shaking. I wanted a desolate street, empty of noise and sound and breath, wiped of witnesses. I wanted someone to hold my hand. I wanted not to hate these children.

Beside the school was Avi's apartment building. The front was pitted brown brick, old and crumbling, with wide front doors edged in wood painted a deep cream with red striping. But she'd told me to come in the back, where wooden fire escape stairs climbed, twisted and doubled back on themselves. I ascended to the middle floor, counted down three doors, and knocked while the world skipped a beat.

The door swung open, and Avi stood there, leaning her hip against the splintered and scratched wood frame, her head tipped to the side, dark hair springing out from the elastic at the end of her braid and curling against the green cotton of her T-shirt. She smiled with only one corner of her mouth, the lip of the opposite corner caught between her teeth.

I tightened my grip on my bag, and shifted it higher onto my shoulder. I thought there'd be an explosion of stars in my head. I thought the sudden physical presence of her would blow out all the windows inside me, leaving the ground sharp and glinting, leaving me paralyzed, stupid, ragged.

It should have happened that way. But the dumb body ticks along. Blood slips through veins, breath is drawn in and eased out, the reptile brain flicks its small slow tail, and one moment in time slips over into the next. I willed my fingers to relax, and held my hands out to her.

"Avi, hey. Jesus. You haven't changed at all." That was a lie. It'd been nine years.

She took my hands and pulled me toward her, backing up as she did so that we didn't touch, but we both moved into her apartment. It smelled of incense and coffee. The windows were covered in tied-together swaths of lavender satin. I caught a glimpse of the living room as she pulled me, by one hand, toward the kitchen: Indian and African cloth thrown over the furniture, photos on the walls framed in bamboo, a woven screen in the corner, bright things of painted wood on the tables. A white and black cat under a chair, its green eyes wide.

"I made coffee," she said. "I don't really drink it anymore, but I thought, What the hell, right? If all the coffee we drank before didn't kill us both, another cup for old time's sake will be fine." She paused in the doorway to her kitchen and looked up at me for a long moment. I stood very still and tried to empty my face of expression, but I could feel my shoulders pulling back, my spine clicking into place, drawing me upwards.

"Sit, go ahead," she said, gesturing toward the kitchen table. The table was smooth dark wood, elaborately carved around the edges, with a roughly textured orange and purple runner bisecting the length of it. The chairs were wooden and mismatched, each painted a different colour with hand-drawn wildflowers twining around the seats. I sat down on a yellow one covered in tiny purple crocuses with my back to the wall as she turned toward the counter and the coffee pot.

"It's really good to see you," she said after she turned away. Her voice sounded small, and she ran her hand over her hair, just the way she'd done a million times before, usually when she wasn't sure about something. Or when she was lying. My legs lifted a few centimetres, trying to stand, but I pressed my spine back down into the chair and leaned down to stuff my bag behind my feet. "I don't really have sugar in the house," she said, walking toward me with grey cups in each hand, "but you take it black anyway, right?"

I didn't take it black, not anymore. Somewhere along the line I'd discovered how much better coffee tasted with sugar, and thick cream, and kicked myself for all those years of swallowing sharp black coffee late into the night, my tongue scalded and my breath bitter.

"It's fine, hon," I said, and positioned my mouth into something that I hoped looked like a smile. And then I realized what I'd called her, old patterns of tongue and teeth emerging, record player needles slipping thoughtlessly into familiar grooves. She looked at me, her brown eyes startled, and then her fingers started nervously pulling at the edges of the runner, smoothing and straightening what was already perfectly smooth, perfectly straight. I wanted to grab her hands and squeeze, until her silver rings cut into her long perfect fingers, until she made a small noise in the bottom of her throat. Until I could breathe again. Until I knew if I wanted to get up and walk back out the door, or stay here a while longer, hovering at the edges of her kitchen, waiting to see what she'd wanted to say to me.

"Wow," she said softly. "Intense, huh?" She looked up at me again, and then stared down into her coffee. "So, what? Eight years? What have I missed?" She smiled. "What have you been up to?"

This game, I thought. The snapshot synopsis of years of absence. Fifty words or less — the high school reunion special.

"Nine years, Avi," I said quietly. Nine years in September, anyway. Nine fucking years. I wanted to lunge across the room and grab her small shoulders in my fingers, shake her and shake her. I wanted her to tangle her arms around my neck and pull until I disappeared inside of her. I wanted to fall into a messy knot on her kitchen floor and weep until I floated away. I wanted this all to be a memory of something that had already happened and I wanted, desperately, to never find out for sure what happened next.

I took a breath, rubbed my hands against my jeans, and pulled up what I hoped was a bright smile from someplace sticky inside. "Well. I don't know. I went to university, got involved with the Women's Centre. Went out to Vancouver for a couple of years, but everyone was too laid-back, you know? I came back here, graduated, and I've been working with Nine Circles since then. Community health outreach stuff." I took a sip of coffee. "It's burn-out work. I know that. But I like it. I like feeling that some days, some little thing that I do makes a difference to someone. That probably sounds cheesy."

"No," she said. "Sounds good." She ran her finger around and around the rim of her coffee cup. There was a small silence in the room, and the clock ticked and the walls bent imperceptibly outward.

"What about you, Av?" I asked. "What happened after you went to Israel?" Because that was all I knew. She'd gone to Israel.

I hadn't heard from her for a couple of weeks. When I'd tried to call her apartment, the number was no longer in service. I'd finally called her parents' place after I'd looked up their number in the phone book, my hands shaking with exhaustion and a deep fear that kept my tendons stretched and humming. I had the phone pressed too tightly against my ear, and when her father answered his deep rumble made my head ache. *Avital's not here*, he'd said. *She's in Israel. Who's calling?* Israel? I'd whispered. I told him my name. *She never mentioned you*, he'd said. *I don't know when she's coming back. I'm sure she'll call.*

And that was it. For weeks I didn't go out at all. I stayed in my apartment, and I didn't even talk to my roommates. They were good about it. Every now and then they'd knock on my bedroom door. When I opened it no one was there, but there'd be a cup of tea and a bagel or a slice of pizza on a plate in the hallway. Mostly I just sat on my bed and smoked cigarettes. I spread out all the T-shirts and scarves and random bits of things that she'd left at my place, all over my bed, and then I laid down on top of them and slept. It was awful, and ridiculous. When I couldn't smell her on her clothes anymore, when they only smelled like smoke and sweat, I started to panic. And then things got dark. I started to think about suicide bombers. I started to envision scenarios in my head. Avi walking through a market place, swinging her bag. Avi sitting at a roadside table, at a café, laughing and tilting her head. Smiling, at a boy. And then the suicide bomber walking up the road, not looking at anything, not looking at Avi and the boy, but stopping in front of them, looking up, taking a full breath, shouting something maybe. And then, what? Pressing a button? Disconnecting a wire? I didn't really know how it worked. But then the terrible sound, sound that tore up bones and tissue, sound that filled up the whole street, the world, and then ripped them apart. And the terrible sight of the world flying apart, too fast to track, like my own mind exploding. Things that were cars, now just metal projectiles. Things that were tables and chairs and pots of flowers, now just nothing. And in the middle of the explosion, in the middle of the noise that tore out eardrums, in the street turned red and orange, was Avi, screaming.

Usually screaming my own name.

And the sound of my name, in her voice, circled tight with terror, was all that I could hear in my head. And I knew I had to get out.

I started going, obsessively, to all the places we'd gone

together. I sat by the window in Cousin's, my leg jostling up and down, watching the door. I drank black coffee in The Nook until they kicked me out. I spent my evenings at Tubby's, drinking beer, waiting for Burton Cummings to come in and play the slots. I sat on the swings in Central Park, making myself small and angry, and even the dealers left me alone. I spent a whole Saturday riding the number ten bus around and around its route, walking to the front and dropping a ticket in every time we passed the St. B. When the bus finished its last loop for the night, I got out at Aubrey Park and sat under the suspension bridge of the play structure and smoked a joint.

When I stumbled home that night, my roommates had had enough. I'd had just about all I could take of myself, too. Shel and Lisa shoved me into the shower until all the accumulated grime sluiced away down the drain. Then they sat with me at the kitchen table with a bottle of Jägermeister and a row of shot glasses and demanded that I talk. I wouldn't, at first. I was too tightly coiled. But they kept pouring me shots of Jäger and asking stupid questions, and eventually I did talk. And then I couldn't stop talking. I even told them about the suicide bomber fantasy. Lisa just grabbed my shoulders and kissed the top of my head and poured me another shot. *Drink, dammit!* she said, and I did. The night ended as dawn slid up the side of our apartment building, cold and grey, while the three of us stood in the lane and hurled every dish that we owned at the yellow brick, cheering madly at each crash and shatter.

The next day I bought a new set of dishes at Value Village. I quit smoking. And I started to get it together, to pull the skin tight over the throbbing, aching little place inside me. Shel helped me get a new job at a restaurant across town. Lisa dragged me out with her friends every night until I surprised myself by enjoying them. And, in the way that these things go, the ache ached less, the throb throbbed less, until eventually, when it flared up in tiny streaks inside me, for a quick moment I couldn't even remember anymore what it was all about. My body kept walking through the world, one foot after another, and so did I.

I used to know this girl named Avi, I'd say sometimes. *I don't know whatever happened to her, but there was this one time....* She was just another story that I told.

"So, Av?" I asked, looking at her face, but not her eyes, looking instead at the little strands of hair that twisted around her forehead and above her ears. "When did you get back to Winnipeg?"

She took a breath and reached her hand toward me. I didn't move, and her hand faltered and came to rest on the glossy table, halfway between us. "Six years ago," she said, and looked away, over my head. She didn't say anything else, and I turned my head to see what she was looking at. Another photo, another bamboo frame. This one was of Avi, smiling with her lopsided lips, her hair loose and curling over her shoulders. On her shoulder was a hand, a boy's hand, attached to an arm and a body and a boy's face. Maybe a man's face, smiling goofily down at her, his eyes soft.

"That's Jacob," she said softly. "We met in Israel, on a kibbutz, but he's actually from here too. Amazing, huh?" I didn't say anything. My body felt like steel, and my mouth like sandpaper. "When we left Israel we travelled around for a year or so... Africa, India, Thailand, Cambodia. A little bit of Europe. Mostly just Paris and Vienna, and the train in between. He's an architect, and we just wanted to, I don't know, see stuff. And then we came home, because our families are here. And then three years ago we got married. It was just time, you know?" I was still turned, staring at the photo, but I could feel her eyes looking straight at me. "I thought it was time," she said. "I thought that marriage was the right thing to do."

I closed my eyes, my body still turned away from her. The world inside my eyes was dark, darker than coffee, darker than parks at night, darker than the inside of the lizard's throat, and streaked with a dull red. *Six years*, I thought. *Marriage*, I thought. Disembodied words lifted up through my throat, mechanical words with sharp edges. "Really," I said. "I guess I never thought of you as the marrying kind, Avi." I opened my eyes and looked at her. My throat was as cold and slick as the inside of a steel pipe. Her face was completely still, the dark edges of her eyebrows lifted away from the edges of her eyes like little wings snapped mid-flight. "I guess I never thought of you as the kind of girl who makes those kinds of promises. And then keeps them. I never thought of you as that kind of woman, Avi." I paused. "When I thought of you at all, that is." I couldn't look at her face anymore, her small white rigid face. I lifted my eyes to the wall behind her head, traced a long thin crack in the plaster, waited for the sharp icy edges of my tongue to melt back into something soft, something warm, something I could bear to have in my mouth. The silence pushed at my ears like shock waves.

"I'm sorry," she said, so softly I almost couldn't hear her at all. I didn't say anything. I just waited and breathed. "Are you married?" she asked.

I pushed my body back into my chair and it scraped abruptly backwards along the kitchen floor, a small terrible sharp sound that made me wince, the sound of a tear, a rip in something fragile. "No, Avi," I said. "I'm not married."

The lashes around her eyes looked blacker. That meant, I remembered, that she was about to cry. "I thought it was the right thing to do. Look, you're right. When you make a promise to someone, you should keep it." She leaned forward. I stayed very still. "Whatever promises I've made, I meant. I meant to say them, and I meant to keep them. It's just... sometimes it's hard, you know?" She dropped her eyes, and pulled at the end of her braid. "Sometimes you don't know what you want. And sometimes you think you know what you want, but once you really have it, it's not what you wanted at all. Sometimes you don't know what you want until you don't have it anymore. Do you know what I mean?"

"Avi, look at me," I said. I held myself very still and taut. She slowly lifted her eyes. Each of our separate bodies stayed perfectly motionless. The clock on her stove ticked in the silence, interminable spaces between the small sharp shots.

The back of my head began to buzz. "Avi, why did you call me? After all this time, all this time you've been here. Six years you've been back, Av. Jesus, six years! Why did you ask me to come over today?"

She looked behind me again, at the wall behind my head. At the photo. She pulled the elastic off the end of her hair and started to unbraid it, pulling her fingers through the snarls. A tiny piece of me tumbled forward into the soft brown tangle and disappeared. I wondered, briefly, if there were scissors in reach, saw the glint of silver as they sliced through the brown mass, heard the rasp of hair against metal as something severed and fell away.

You can't put it back together again, I thought. You can grieve and you can rage and you can want it so hard that you're bleeding inside. After the world blows up it goes on anyway, and the muscles of the heart keep plodding and the lizard keeps blinking and things go on, but they don't go back together. Not the way they were.

When she opened her mouth to speak, her voice shook and she cleared her throat a few times. "I'm sorry. I'm sorry, okay? I just... it was just hard. With you, it was just so... so much. I wasn't exactly ready, and I didn't know how to feel so much. So I told my parents I needed to go to Israel. Of course they were thrilled, and I didn't really know how to do the whole goodbye thing, so I just left. It was stupid and immature. And hurtful. For me, too, you know. It hurt me. And then I met Jacob and it just felt easy. And everyone was so happy for me. My family. And Jacob's a really good guy, you know? He is.

He's good to me." She leaned forward and put her palms on my knees and I felt the skin begin to tear, the skin that had grown so tight and smooth and shiny, like a scar. "But he's not what I want," she said steadily, her voice low. "I want something else."

She had tiny lines around her eyes, I saw, lines that didn't used to be there. They were beautiful. I remembered how her hair felt, loose and tangled and wiry against my bare shoulder. I remembered how still she could hold herself, and then how fast she could move, like electricity leapt through her muscles.

"I remembered something," I said. "I remembered to bring you something."

I leaned down and grabbed my bag from where I'd shoved it behind my chair. I pulled a plastic LC bag out of it, and handed it to her. She took it from me, hesitantly. "You brought me something?" she asked. I nodded, and she reached into the bag, and pulled out a small candle holder. It was pewter, and big enough to hold a votive. Attached to the base was a coloured glass screen for the candle to shine through. She held it up to the afternoon light coming in her kitchen window. The yellow glass shone around the edges. In the middle were green leaves outlined in the dark dull metal, and a white horse with wings, the glass milky. "It's pretty," she said, and smiled.

"Yeah. It is pretty," I said slowly. "Actually, it's from my parents. They went to Boston the week before you went away. They bought it for you. I was kind of mad, actually. I hadn't decided if I was really going to give it to you or not.

And then. Well. You were gone anyway." I paused, and breathed, and the walls exhaled and stood straighter.

She leaned forward, the little candle holder still in her hand. In the window light it had shone, for a moment. In her hand, out of the light, it looked silly. Tacky. Something that, when I was twenty, I'd thought was beautiful. Something that I'd grown out of. I thought of my apartment, all clean lines and pop art prints on the walls, retro dykey Ann Bannon magnets on the fridge. There wasn't anywhere that I could put a candle holder with a winged horse on it. I thought of that pile of broken dishes behind my old apartment building. I thought of the dinner party I was going to later in the evening, all the women that would be there — still Shel and Lisa, of course, and women I'd met through them, through university, through work. Women I knew all the way through, and women I wanted to know more about, to sit up with all night, asking questions and drinking wine and laughing together. Women to make new stories with. The candle holder would blend into Avi's folky wood and paint and purple-scarved apartment and maybe the wings would fold over her sad little heart. Or maybe she'd knock it off the edge of a table one day and the coloured glass would shatter against the floor and she'd just sweep it up and throw it away and never think of it again. Either way, it wasn't mine to hang onto anymore. And a tiny flash in the back of my head wondered why I'd kept it for so long in the first place.

"But listen..." she started.

I reached out and cupped her face. My palms burned.

"Avi," I said. I took my hands away, reached down for my bag, and stood up. "I'm glad you called me," I said. "I hope you find what you're looking for." I started to walk down her hallway. When I reached her back door, I felt her grab my hand behind me. "Wait," she said. Her voice was tinny around the edges. "Maybe you don't understand what I mean," she said, her fingers like vises around mine.

"I do understand. I really do. But it's not a good idea. You should talk to your husband. Or your friends. You always had lots of friends, right? Or go to therapy or something. I don't know." I pulled my hand out of her grip. "I just...." I leaned my head against the doorframe. "When you called, I didn't know what to think. But I wanted to know what happened. But sometimes... sometimes you see a road you haven't been down in years, somewhere that you really loved. And you think about walking down it again, for old time's sake, to feel that again, you know? Except it's... I don't know. It's not what you remembered, exactly. The houses are all different colours, the wrong people are sitting on the steps. Or it's the wrong time of year and none of the trees are flowering. Or maybe you don't even like those kinds of trees anymore, maybe they just give you a headache. Or maybe, I don't know. Maybe the road's not even really there anymore. Maybe something bad happened and everything just blew away and collapsed. Which is sad, totally sad, but it's fine. Because what's important about it is always in your head anyway. But the road itself, and all the stuff it used to hold in the world... it's just gone." I closed my eyes. "God, that's dumb. I'm not saying this well at all."

"Yeah," she said, and I could hear the smile in her throat. "That's fucking stupid." I opened my eyes and looked at her. She was smiling. I grinned, unexpectedly, and my face didn't break. She put her arms around my neck, hard, and pulled me into her. "Fucking chicken soup for the fucking soul," she whispered. I wrapped my arms around her back, felt the warmth and moisture of her skin through her T-shirt. "Goodbye, Avi," I said, holding the doorknob in my hand.

"Fuck you," she said, her voice soft. She reached up and kissed my cheek, and then let go. Her eyelashes were dark against her skin, but she was still smiling.

I opened the door and stepped outside. I walked back down the wooden fire stairs and around to the front of the building. I wasn't sure which window would be hers from this angle. The crossing guards weren't back out yet; they were tucked away in their classrooms in the beautiful white school, running down the hallway bathed in red and blue from the sun shining through the window. Maybe some of them noticed it. One day when they were older they'd walk past the school and remember the light, have a vague visceral memory of being small and lovely and protected. And then a car would drive by or a bird would rustle or they'd remember that they needed to get coffee at the store and they'd forget what they were remembering, and look up to the sun, the real sun, bright and steady on their skin.

Walking at night, in winter, in steel-toed boots, is more of a slide than a step, each foot thankful for every remaining patch of sand that stops your foot short and anchors you to this snow, this sidewalk, this frozen ground beneath. I can feel the skin on my thighs going numb and papery under my jeans, and the cold from the steel in my boots seeps into my toes. I try to keep them pressed to the soles, try not to let them lift up to the top of the boots. My toes clench like I'm walking on sand, and I try to hold sand in my mind: beach sand, swimsuit sand, warm sand. Not city sand dumped instead of salt on moonlit winter sidewalks, the pavement suffocating four inches underneath, each molecule grasping the other with outstretched arms as the concrete slowly dreams of cracking in the spring.

I am walking home from my mother's apartment. I feel slightly queasy from cheesecake, my blood sluggish and sweet, the inside of my throat raw from sugar and chocolate. My mother calls about once a week, says, *Let's go somewhere.* She always buys. I'm always broke. She wants someone to talk to about her boyfriend. We have the same conversation over and over. She tells me whatever stupid or thoughtless or cruel or ridiculous thing he's done. I tell her he's an alcoholic. I tell her about abuse cycles. I offer to draw her the circle: the build-up, the crisis, the honeymoon.

I should know. But we don't really talk about me. We

should all know better. Maybe we do know better. Knowing doesn't seem to make a difference. I don't know what will. I long for a window, a bird inside my ribs, someone with a car and a lot of money. I long to unzip myself and just walk out like a cartoon wolf in sheep's clothing.

I love this pause, this cold walk in the dark between my mother's apartment and my own. I pass the occasional person with their dog, the occasional couple leaning into each other, but everyone has hats and hoods and scarves wrapped around their faces and it's impossible to recognize anyone, too cold to stop and talk even if you do. I love the way the snow glitters in this kind of cold, multifaceted like shattered glass, glinting in the pools of streetlights. I love staring unabashedly into people's windows as I walk past their houses, imagining myself in that red living room, staring at that framed and glassed piece of yellow and blue art, moving out of sight into the kitchen to get a fresh cup of coffee or velvety glass of wine, surrounded by other people and staring out the window. Unable to see anything past the reflected glare of lamps in the giant square windows, unable to see me standing on the sidewalk, longing and looking in, leftover Christmas lights still outlining the edges of the houses in blue and red.

I always arrive at my apartment building too soon, but still just past the moment when I can't stand the cold any longer, when the scarf over my mouth is simultaneously damp and frozen and smells like my breath, when my armpits are clammy under my coat and my legs and fingers are stiff and screaming. Letters are missing from the arch over the doorway so that it reads *Do   le* instead of *Dorvale.* My boyfriend Mike thinks that's funny. Almost everyone who lives here is on welfare, including us. The walls are cracked and the hallways smell and there are no showers, only old stained tubs, and we've only ever seen the landlord twice and both times he was yelling, but the rent is cheap and you can make as much noise as you want. Generally everyone minds their own business, although someone always lets the cops in the locked front door.

The cops have shown up at our door a few times but I always tell them that we were watching a movie too loud or that the guy who called them is schizophrenic and off his head. I am polite and make a smile look genuine. They leave and I am filled with relief and self-loathing and I grab another beer and the evening carries on the way it always does.

The door to my apartment is unlocked, but Mike's not there. I take off my gloves and unwrap my scarf and hang my coat on one of the big brass hooks by the door. I pour myself a generous glass of Jim Beam, and stand as close as I can to the radiator in the living room. The bourbon is the colour of mud through the blue glass and I take small sips at first, warming my lips. I open my throat and down the rest of the glass, and I am suddenly aware of the passages and tunnels in my body, lit up and flaming. Artificial warmth spreads through my body and I can feel the tendons in my neck loosening.

I grab the bottle of JB from the kitchen and sit at the end of the brown couch, still near the radiator, and wrap myself in the ratty old red and black afghan. With one hand I pour another glass, with the other I dial my mother's number.

Hey. I'm home. She always wants me to call to make sure I haven't been raped and murdered on the short walk home from her place. It's too cold for rape or murder but my connection with her is so fragile and tenuous, despite our coffee and cheesecake meetings. I feel like she's out in space, spinning a million miles away from me. I feel like she tries, but I'm invisible to her, messy hair, dirty jeans, a yellow cheekbone the mirror image of hers. I feel like I could be anyone at all sitting across the table from her and she wouldn't notice, couldn't tell the difference. She doesn't always answer the phone and sometimes I just leave a message which she never returns, but tonight she picks up and I can hear something breaking in the background.

What? Oh, good. Listen, I have to go. The cat's going crazy.

I know it's not the cat, but it doesn't matter what I know or what I say. She'll tell me everything about her relationship — the drinking, the sex, the fighting, the exact word-for-word replay of their arguments, but she'll never tell me about him hitting her. Or pushing or kicking or whatever goes on over there. Once the hospital called me. It was summer, and I ran the whole twelve blocks. When I got there she had a cast on her arm and a split lip. She was furious the nurse had called me. She said she was fine. She said she tripped over the cat and fell. *Your cat is fucked up,* I told her. I fall a lot too.

Okay, Mom, I say. *Be safe.* She's already hung up. I put the phone back on the receiver and take another sip. My throat burns in that old familiar way, and I take another.

It's good to have the apartment to myself, no punk rock crashing, no breaking glass, no tightening in my chest. I am lulled by the silence, by the drink in my hand. I light a smoke and blow lazy smoke rings into the air, sticking my lips out like a round duck bill, pushing from my throat. Mike is most likely over at Jesse's place, drinking beer and watching Monty Python, reciting all the words along with the movie, passing a joint back and forth. It's what they always do. Then later they'll start fucking around with Jesse's computer, taking things apart and putting them back together just to see how they work, old motherboards and hard drives piled on the kitchen table like space junk. I could go down the hall and join them, but it's boring. I used to think Monty Python was funny, but after seeing all the movies a million times they've lost their charm. And computers bore me to tears. I can't imagine what I'd use a computer for. No one I know has email. There's nothing I want to look up and I'm happy playing solitaire with real cards.

Leftover rolls of Christmas paper lean against the wall behind the couch. I wish we'd had a tree this year. We've never had a tree in all the three years Mike and I have been together. They're too expensive, and we don't have any of the things you need for a tree, the stand or the ornaments or lights. We don't have a car so we wouldn't even be able to get one home, even if we wanted to. Usually I don't really care. Christmas isn't a big deal around here. Mike's mom sends a card from Surrey with a cheque for twenty-five dollars in it, every year. His dad is long gone, working somewhere up north maybe. My dad calls on Christmas morning at ten exactly. He uses his cell phone and I can hear his wife and her kids in the background, clearing up the dishes, toys crashing and honking and beeping. He says, *Merry Christmas*, and, *How are you?* and I say, *Yeah, you too,* and, *I'm fine, how's Wendy?* and then we don't have much else to say. We go to Mom's for dinner and she cooks up the Cheer Board chicken I bring over. Her boyfriend is at home with his wife so it's pretty quiet. We all end up drinking too much and Mike and I fall down in the snow all the way home, and then we have drunk sex and go to sleep.

When I was little Christmas was different. I guess it's always different when you're little, waiting for Santa and stockings and special eggs and bacon for breakfast. I always had a new nightgown for Christmas Eve and Mom and Dad slept together down the hall, although later my mom slept on the couch, and then after that she slept in her bedroom and Dad slept at Wendy's. And then Mom sold the house altogether, and she got her apartment and I moved in with Mike.

But I still try to give presents, even though they're dumb things like cookies I made or candles from the dollar store that smell so strong that they give you a headache, even through the paper. And Mike tries to give me something every year, even though this year he had to pawn the Nintendo to buy me the Clash T-shirt I'm wearing under my hoodie. I gave him a bottle of Jägermeister and the Union

Jack flag he hung up in the living room window instead of a curtain.

I pull the flag aside now and see that it's started to snow. I wonder if my mom's looking out her window too, right at this exact moment. *Oh, the weather outside is frightful,* I hum, resting my elbow on the window ledge, the glass of bourbon knocking against my teeth as I drink. I've been drinking steadily, refilling the glass, and I'm slightly drunk now. The snowflakes are fat and lazy. They look like pale round babies rolling around in the sky. They look like drifty tears. They look like frozen butterflies, lolling through the air and disappearing on the ground. There's a tiny flake stuck to the glass, and it looks just like the snowflakes we used to cut out in elementary school with safety scissors and pin around the edges of the bulletin board. It's round with spiky spines sticking out of it, tiny fuzzy snow bridges joining the spines together. It's beautiful and I touch my finger to the cold glass and my eyes burn.

I always fight or cry or fuck when I'm drunk, and tonight I'm crying over snowflakes. I want to be one so badly that I feel like my chest is about to break open, burn, and shrivel up inside me. I want to feel myself spontaneously sprouting eight arms all around my body, cold and perfect and cupped in the black hands of sky. I want to shatter into crystals and glue myself back together again. I want to trip on the wind. I want to look down on the top of this apartment building, the tips of trees. I want to slip through the black lines of telephone wire. I want to have no ears, I want absolute silence. I want to feel nothingness all around me. I want to be attached to nothing, feel nothing pulling on me but wind. I want to land on someone's tongue, their open mouth stretched up to the night. I want them to swallow me and take me somewhere else, somewhere far away. I don't want to belong to anyone. I want to dissolve.

I get scissors from the kitchen. I pull out the rolls of Christmas paper and start cutting. Soon I am completely drunk, my hands are full of tiny red cuts, and the walls are covered with snowflakes made of red Santas on green paper, gold and red stripes, white dogs with red bows and presents. There are shards and fragments of paper all over the floor, and everything on the walls is covered with my clumsy paper flakes, even Mike's punk posters, the Picasso flowers I got at the Sally Ann, the beer labels taped across the back wall. I lie on the sofa with the scissors on my chest and the empty bottle on the floor beside me. I hear Mike stumble in the door and down the hall.

Hey, you home? he slurs from the hallway. I hear him slam against the long white wall and then keep walking, sliding against it. *Your fucking mother called earlier. I'm going to change the number soon. That stupid bitch.* He stops in the living room doorway and looks around. He blinks and says, *What the fuck?*

Fuck you, I say, and close my eyes, floating away.

You're one fucked-up chick, he says, reaching over and pulling down a snowflake, then another.

Merry fucking Christmas, you bastard, I mumble. But it doesn't matter, because I'm already gone.

A BOY WITH PINK LIPSTICK

Langley Properties were buying up all the old apartment buildings in the city and only hired ex-cons to manage them. They'd put a tiny fake wood ceiling fan in the living rooms, and a cheap removable shower head in the old stained claw foot tubs, and call them "remodeled character suites," jacking up the rents. There were still mice and mould and water damage, and I had to call the health department every fall to get them to turn the heat on, but we'd moved into our apartment before Langley bought the building, so the rent was still pretty cheap for us.

Don was our caretaker. I don't know what he'd been in for, but it must have been something serious, because he'd been in for a long time. He was an old guy, his grey hair buzzed close to the scalp, and kind of mean looking. Angry, don't-fuck-with-me looking. But he had a soft spot for girls. He barely acknowledged my boyfriend Mark, but he'd open the door for me if I had groceries. Once I knocked on his door to ask him to tie a tie for me. "Whaddya want?" he'd said when he opened his door, wires of grey hair sticking up out of the neck of his Children's Hospital sweatshirt.

"I don't know how to do this," I'd said, holding out the early 70s purple swirly tie I'd bought at the Sally Ann. "Could you help me?"

He looked at me for a minute, then reached out and flipped up the collar of Mark's dress shirt. His fingers were rough and smelled like tobacco, like when you put a smoke out halfway and put it in your pocket and then you just reek of ashtray and everyone on the bus looks at you like you're a bum. He put the tie around my neck and kind of measured it out, and then twisted it around itself and tied it up. He wasn't gentle, but he wasn't rough either. Then he slid the knot up and flipped the collar down again. He didn't even look at my chest. Just my neck. And he didn't touch me anywhere, just his fingers sliding around the frayed fabric of the white shirt, the shiny lilac rayon of the tie. He tied a knot around my neck as if I were a doll or a block of wood. When he was done I started to say thank you, but he just closed his door. I heard him walking back down his hall, then I heard the tinny TV sounds of a talk show, and that was all.

I didn't usually wear clothes like that. I usually wore skirts and dangly earrings and things with flower prints. Ukrainian scarves with big red roses that looked like tablecloths. I had a long deep blue taffeta skirt that sounded like girls hissing when I walked, and a gold and red tunic with tiny mirrors sewn into the bodice. But I was on my way to Klinic for a pregnancy test, and I didn't want anything with flowers or mirrors or whispers. I wanted to look like a boy. A boy with pink lipstick and chewed-up fingernails.

I was pretty sure that I was pregnant. Like everyone, I'd been pregnant before, and though each time was a little different, there was always more to it than just skipping a period. Little things. barely noticeable spasms in the belly. Always feeling sort of full. Crying too much. Electric sparks of hope, and breath-stealing dread.

So when the nurse at Klinic took me into one of the counselling rooms to tell me that the test was positive, I wasn't really surprised. I cried, of course. She rubbed my knee, and held out a box of tissues, the cheap kind that just disintegrate in your fingers when you try to wipe your eyes or blow your nose. She made the arrangements they always make: for an ultrasound as soon as possible, for an appointment with an actual doctor. She started to talk about options, but I told her I knew what my options were. Morgantaler's on Corydon. Women's Pavilion at Health Sciences. Those were the main ones. There were the various, mostly nebulous adoption options. Or keeping it. Or, at least, thinking about keeping it. Thinking about thinking about it, and waiting to see what would happen. Sixty percent of all pregnancies miscarry in the first trimester. Most of the time you barely even notice.

Klinic was just up on Portage, pretty much around the corner from my building. I pulled open the glass and metal door, walked down the shallow concrete steps under the fan of flags above me, rainbows and leaves and buffalo and the white against blue shock of infinity loops. I stood for a moment on the corner of Portage Avenue, a rush of cars shredding and tearing the thick hot air behind my back. Even from here I could see Mark sitting on the flat concrete steps of the apartment block, smoking a cigarette. Waiting for me. I felt sick all of a sudden, nausea slamming against the back of my throat. Mark, or the baby, or both. *Not baby*, I thought. *Fetus.* A small collection of tissues, pink and hard like a marble in my belly.

I cut across the road to the park across the street, Vimy Ridge Park, with a war memorial and a fenced-in lawn bowling green full of old people moving very slowly, rolling round black balls endlessly up and down the one immaculate green patch in the whole place. Swing sets, a wading pool, picnic tables and rusty barbeque pits and giant sagging trees. At night we called it Rape Ridge Park and stayed the hell away from it. And then the sun would rise up in the morning and lick the gang tags newly graffitied on the play structure and the tired looking moms would show up and set up shop, sitting on the benches and smoking, the kids tearing around and falling down and getting up again.

I sat on a peeling green bench behind some bushes, so that I could see Mark but he couldn't really see me unless he actually looked. I lit a smoke, took a deep drag and felt the nicotine ricochet through my body like fireworks. I held it pinched between my thumb and index finger and took hard drags out of the side of my mouth like I'd seen old men do, sitting for hours at the Albert in the middle of the day. I spread my knees out and sat back easy on my hips on the bench, squinted my eyes and stared up at the sky. Behind me I could hear a kid, a little one, kind of singing and yelling at the same time, and coming closer.

"There was an old woman who swallowed a fly-iy-iy! I guess she'll die-ie-ie!"

A little blond kid stood in front of me in grubby jeans and a yellow T-shirt. Three or four years old, I guessed.

"Was that you singing?" I asked. The kid nodded and stared

at me. "Where'd you learn that song?"

The kid kept staring at me and whispered, "I guess she'll die."

I tipped my head back and closed my eyes. "Maybe she will," I said. "How the fuck do I know."

"Fuck," the kid said.

"Don't swear," I said, and felt like a dick. I used to babysit, once upon a time a million years ago. I used to give kids baths and crackers with peanut butter and teach them how to write their names with big fat crayons. Now look at me.

"What's your name?" I asked.

"Sky."

"Really? Sky? That's great. Are you a boy or a girl, Sky?"

"Are you a boy or a girl?" Sky asked me back.

I thought about it for a minute. "I'm a boy. Can't you tell?"

Sky giggled. "No you're not! You're a girl! Girl! Girl!"

"She's a girl," a man's voice said. I looked over and saw Don standing about ten feet away, smoking a cigarette exactly the way I was trying to do it. He turned his head to the side and spat, a quick, hard shot onto the grass. "Sky's a girl. Come on, kid," he said.

"Uncle Don! Uncle Don!" Sky yelled, and launched herself at him, wrapping her arms around his leg.

"I'm not your uncle," he said, and reached down and slid his hand, slowly, across her hair. She turned her face up to his and grinned like a small dirty daisy, and I felt the nausea reaching its insistent fingers up into my throat again. Across the street, Mark was still sitting on the steps, but he was starting to look pissed off and bored. I figured he'd only hang out for another fifteen minutes, tops, before he took off somewhere else. I decided I could wait him out. I stretched my arms along the length of the top of the bench and closed my eyes, slowed everything down until all I could hear was the tiny whistle in my lungs every time I breathed, in and out.

Mark's jeans, his belt wrapped twice around my hips. Blue dress shirt. White undershirt, also Mark's. No bra, my breasts tight and full and licked beneath with grimy sweat. I sat on the front steps of the building in the four o'clock sunshine, waiting for Mark. I'd forgotten my keys, and Don wasn't answering the buzzer. Small, damp kids in T-shirts and diapers shrieked from the wading pool across the street. The hot sticky air settled its hands around my throat, smelling of car exhaust and cigarettes and flowers I didn't know the names of. I still hadn't told Mark about the maybe-baby. I hadn't said much to him at all over the past few days. It was so unrelentingly hot, all the time, even at night. I couldn't stand anything touching me. Anyone touching me. I'd move Mark's arm off my chest, his skin slick with sweat, the bone inside deadweight with sleep and Wild Turkey. He wouldn't even roll over.

I got up and curled into the ratty wicker chair by the window, my arms wrapped around my pale knees. Mark had pinned a stupid DOA flag to the window frame when we'd moved in, but half of it had been pulled down in some fight ages ago, and neither of us had ever bothered to tack it up again. It hung in a dusty black mass on the left, and the sallow light from the streetlight just outside throbbed slowly through the dirty window. My damp skin glowed like those thick, pulsing fish deep in the ocean when the camera beam hits them. You know that's not how they see themselves. It's not how they see each other. It's just what it looks like on TV, artificial, a cadaverous glimpse. The immense loneliness of that pale alien thing swimming and swimming alone through the endless black ocean just broke my heart, every time I thought about it. I uncurled from the chair, put on my dead grandfather's grey fedora and grabbed a pillow, and climbed into the chair again, the bits of broken wicker snagging my skin. I let myself glow and glow in the flickering electric sheen of the streetlight until I finally fell asleep.

"Hey, spider-kid," I said, holding the front door of the building with my hip and carrying two bags of groceries in one hand as I tried to open the canvas flap of my shoulder bag, stuff my keys inside. Sky didn't say anything, just slowly reached her skinny fingers to her hair, grabbed a long blonde handful, pulled it into her mouth and started sucking on it. She was sitting on the top of the carpeted stairs to the first floor. My apartment was way up at the top, on the third floor. Her pink tank top was inside out. I was tired, and hot, the camo green long johns I'd cut into shorts sticking to the insides of my thighs. I put the plastic bags down on the floor and leaned against the wooden banister, ran my finger through the dust pooled in the gouged-out flower pattern.

The kid made my head hurt, tiny and alone on the stairs, watching me.

"No songs today?" I asked. She shook her head. "Okay. Do you want a banana?" I'd bought fruit at the store. I didn't usually bother with fruit, just loaded up on whatever pasta was on sale. Pasta, rice, soft white bread — anything cheap, anything that sat inside your stomach and slowly expanded, soaking up the acids and black spots and empty places into a tight warm mass. But it was too hot to even boil water in a tin pot on the stove, too hot to put anything warm and soft in my mouth. I wanted things I could eat right away, with just a sharp knife. I wanted to hold something in my hand and slice it open, feel it sigh and split apart in my palm, my fingers sticky.

I reached into the bag and lifted a pale yellow banana off the thick stalk holding them all together. I held it up and showed it to her, and she nodded. "Please," she said. I remembered to break it open for her, peel the thick skin back in strips like flower petals. Little kids' spindly fingers aren't strong enough to do that themselves. The sweet smell of banana filled the hallway, mushy and sickly. The saliva at the back of my mouth pooled into sour acid.

"Oh Christ, here," I said. "Just take the fucking thing." She slid down three steps toward me, slowly reached out her hand, and grabbed it. I put my hand up to my mouth and pressed as hard as I could against my lips, mashing them into my teeth. *Breathe*, I thought. Breathe. Sky stared at me with big speckled eyes, and then turned and ran up the stairs and down the hallway, her sandals flapping. She opened the door at the end of the hall on the left and slammed it behind her. Not Don's apartment; somewhere else. I could almost see the sludgy smell of the banana wavering in the air behind her, a trail, a map, a thick yellow marker line pointing to her bony back on the other side of the apartment door. I sat down on the stairs and put my head between my knees, breathed in the sharp smell of my own sweat. Stared at the too-long laces wrapped around and around the top of my boots. Closed my stupid, stupid eyes that were suddenly wet and burning all at the same time.

Nine in the morning. I'd been awake for hours, watched through the window as the sun lifted up over the park across the street, the green smudgy tips of the trees illuminated in pink fire. My grandpa's striped pajama pants were tied in a knot at my waist to keep them up, and I'd thrown on Mark's old Mentors T-shirt, the one he'd ripped the sleeves off of. It drooped down under my armpits and I kept my arms tight to my body to keep my breasts from showing through. I was sitting on the top of the smelly carpeted stairs outside our apartment, my knees tight up against my chest. Behind me I heard the door open and then close again, and without looking I could feel Mark sitting down beside me, his body radiating heat, his breath stale.

"What the fuck are you doing out here?" he asked, yawning.

"Thinking about throwing myself down the stairs," I said, staring at the ragged tips of my toenails.

"Cool," he said. "Can I watch?"

"I don't think it would work," I said. "It's not a straight drop. I'd have to figure out how to get myself around the corners."

"You'd lose momentum," he said, and lit a cigarette. I heard the scrape of metal as he flicked the Zippo open, heard the hiss of the flame hit the twist of paper at the top of the smoke, the sizzle as the tobacco lit. My head filled and swelled and thudded with the dirty grey smoke.

"Don't you want to know why I'm thinking about throwing myself down the stairs?" I asked.

He took a drag. "I want to throw myself down the fucking stairs every fucking day, babe," he answered. "And quit wearing my fucking clothes. What's the matter with you lately?" He got up and slammed back into the apartment.

"I don't want to clean up your mess," a voice said below me. I shifted my body over and looked between the banisters. Don was standing on the second floor landing, slowly rubbing a dirty cloth up and down the top of the railing. The heat of the day was rising, collecting and pooling around my hunched body. My head felt tiny, muffled in blackness, compressed and aching. "Do it somewhere else, girlie," he said. I heard his footsteps thudding back down the stairs.

"Hey, Uncle Don," I whispered into the tops of my knees. I sat up and the blackness sat up with me. "Uncle fucking Don," I said, out loud. He didn't answer. I heard a car screech at the stop sign on the street below, pause, and take off again.

A couple days later as I was walking down the stairs, my boots unlaced and clomping, my hair shoved up underneath a sweat-stained baseball cap, I saw Sky standing at the top of the landing on the first floor, kicking the banister. She was wearing the same pink tank top, right way out this time, with a long ragged red streak down the front. Jam, probably. Or old ketchup. I sat down on one of the steps and watched her for a minute, the rubber tip of her sandal hitting the wood over and over.

"Doesn't that hurt?" I asked.

She stopped and looked up at me. "Banana girl," she said.

Boy, I thought. *Girl. Boy. Whatever.* I'd eaten nothing but a couple of crackers, but I felt full and heavy. A giant jagged stone. An uneven tree stump, crawling with mites. "I don't have any bananas today," I said. I spread my hands out wide, my fingers stretched. "I don't have anything." She stared at me for a few seconds and started kicking again. Thump. Thump. Like a headache, like a rusty swingset, like a heart.

"Where's Don?"

"Uncle Don sleeping."

"Okay, how's this? Where's your mom? Do you have a mom?"

"Mama working," she said, kicking, kicking.

I didn't have room in my heart for this dirty little kid. My tight black little heart was slowly liquefying and I was just fucking leaking everywhere, and I didn't have room for anything. I sighed, and put my head down on my knees. "I have bananas upstairs," I said. "Do you want one? I could get it and bring it down to you."

I heard her stop kicking, and then felt a small sticky

warmth on the top of my head, right through the cap. "Please," she said. And everything, everything black and dark and rotting inside me lifted right up through my body to that place of warmth, that clumsy little hand that reached for me and just touched me. Just fucking got me. I reached up, put my own hand on top of her small grimy fingers, her delicate little bird bones, and held on, an entire black ocean of quiet around our two separate bodies, the strong white bones inside my fingers glowing and pulsing steadily.

And then everything sped up. The door at the end of the hallway opened, and Sky took off running down the hall, yelling, "Mama!" I looked up, and Mark was walking out of Sky's apartment, grinning, easing his belt into the buckle. Sky disappeared into the apartment. Mark looked up and saw me sitting on the stairs, frozen in the dull heat of the afternoon, looking at him. His face fell, just a little, and then captured itself again. And I knew, I just knew. I knew exactly what kind of work Sky's mother did, why the kid was wandering around the park with Don at weird hours, hanging around the hallways, waiting for her mom to finish. I knew why Mark didn't answer the buzzer when I forgot my keys; he wasn't in our apartment at all. I knew why it was that at night, in bed, he dropped his hot dead arm on top of me like my own body was just a pile of sheets bunched and tangled up in the corner of his world.

I started shaking and I tried to hold myself rigid, tough, like the war statue in the park, like the broken old men in the bar who never spilled a drop of draft. But my stupid, soft, giveaway chin started trembling, and although I was biting my bottom lip hard enough to cut small red lines in the pink flesh, I couldn't stop my traitor eyes from leaking.

Mark stood in front of me and watched me for a moment. "Jesus," he said. "Don't be such a fucking chick." He dropped his hand on top of my head for a quick second, like a hot hairy spider, reeking of perfume and sex, and then lifted his hand away, kept walking up the stairs. "It's not like I paid for it," his voice continued behind me. "Couldn't help giving me a freebie. You gave it away for a session with my stash in Jackie's basement, remember?" I could hear him standing in front of our apartment door, at the top of the stairs. His voice dropped like a rock through the stairwell. I could feel its weight free-falling through space toward my all soft, shaking flesh. "Self-righteous slut," I heard him say, and then the slam of the apartment door. And then nothing.

I didn't, I thought. *It wasn't the pot, you fucking, fucking asshole. It was just you.*

I went to the park, sat in the sticky thrumming green grass with the kids and the moms and the buzzing crawling insects. I waited until I saw Mark take off down the street to the Albert, hours later. I went up to the apartment, changed my clothes, stuffed a bunch of apples in my canvas bag, and went back to the park, the far side where I usually didn't sit. My hands clenched my skirt and left wrinkled sweat stains on the yellow silk. I was back in my own clothes, fabric made from kisses and flicks of the tongue, tiny frayed straps that skimmed my shoulders, the camisole falling around my body like broken butterfly wings. I smoked cigarettes and stared at the blue sky until my mind was blank, reptilian, thick and clotted with knots and blood and breath that didn't move all the way through me. I heard a kid that might have been Sky, with some guy that might have been Don, but I didn't bother looking, just curled myself tighter against the ridges of a thick scarred tree. I sat there all night, watching the streetlights, wishing for stars.

ACKNOWLEDGEMENTS

Thanks and debts of gratitude and great love to Andy Brown, Julika Mayor, Lynn Merrian, David Mayor and Pat Wally, Karen Paquin and Sadie the concierge, Matthew Mayor, Monique Perro, Kier-La Janisse, Allison Crilly, Rachel Stone, Judith Anderson and Becky Hardie, jenn Gusberti, Lindsey Seller and Laura Daniel, Kirsten Brooks, Leslie Braun, Ruth DyckFehderau, Catherine Hunter, Colin Smith, Krishna Lalbiharie, Clare Lawlor, Roewan Crowe, Christine Neufeld, Anita Daher, Bonnie Marin, Sandra Birdsell, Shawna Dempsey and the Spinsters Club, all the *Prairie Fire* folk, and Tannis Gretzinger and all the lovely Millennium librarians and writers. Special thanks to the Millennium Library Writer-in-Residence program, the Manitoba Arts Council, the people who made Scrabulous, and all the bright and shiny everywhere.

Chandra Mayor is the author of *Cherry*, a novel about the Winnipeg skinhead scene in the 1990s, which was nominated for the Margaret Laurence Award for Fiction, and won the Carol Shields Winnipeg Book Award in 2005. Her writing also won the 2004 Manitoba Book Award for Most Promising Writer, and her book of poetry, *August Witch*, was nominated for four Manitoba Book Awards, and won the Eileen McTavish Sykes Award for Best First Book. She was the 2006/07 Writer-in-Residence at the Winnipeg Millennium Library, and was the regional winner of the CBC Poetry Face-Off in 2006 and 2007. Her writing has appeared in the anthologies *Between Interruptions: 30 Women Tell the Truth About Motherhood*, *Breathing Fire 2: Canada's New Poets*, and *Post-Prairie*. She often teaches creative writing workshops and courses and performs at venues and festivals across the country, largely because it means that she gets to leave her house and the incessant barking of her dogs. She also thinks that knitting is entirely sensible and achingly boring, and not particularly radical.